D0120829

The Nuremberg Puzzle

Laurence O'Bryan

Ardua Publishing
5 Dame Lane,
Dublin 2,
Ireland
http://arduapublishing.com

Ordering Information: Contact the publisher.

Paperback Edition, 2017.

ISBN: 978-0-9932425-1-9

"Shake your chains to earth like dew
Which in sleep had fallen on you -
Ye are many - they are few."

Percy Bysshe Shelley
The Masque of Anarchy, 1819

1

Prickling moved up Doctor Brandt's nostrils. He'd been right. It had worked perfectly.

The Plexiglas window was half an inch thick. No sound could be heard from the clean room beyond the glass. There wouldn't be much noise, anyway. The ten-year-old boy lying on the stainless steel gurney was barely breathing, and the blood oozing from his orifices would create only the faintest dripping noise as it fell on the powder-blue floor tiles.

The boy had pulled at the leather straps holding him down when the doctor entered the room. As he'd stared, owl-eyed, at doctor Brandt he'd whispered the only word in English he seemed to know – *father* – before the doctor gave him the injection.

Doctor Brandt had whispered in the boy's ear. He wouldn't have understood the words, but he'd have understood the bed side tone.

Orphans were easy to fool, and there were so many these days. You could take your pick.

The Russian boy in the next experiment room was sleeping peacefully, his skin pearly white against the green sheet, his blond hair draped over his forehead. The contrast with the boy in the other room was striking. The Syrian boy's hair was midnight black. Blood matting into it gave it a fiery sheen.

He checked his watch again. It was well over three hours since the boys had been injected. The results were indisputable. Europe's future was assured.

He walked to the end of the concrete passageway, pressed the switches to pump the air from both experiment rooms. Then he flipped the switches to turn the lights out behind him.

He closed the steel door firmly. There would be no squeamishness.

"Dritten mal glück," he whispered, to himself. Third time lucky.

He glanced again at his watch. The sweeping silver second hand crawled across the black face. It would take the pumps all of sixty seconds to extract the oxygen from the rooms. Death would come within another five minutes, as the boys' lungs imploded.

He walked to the glass door that separated the test facility from the production area. There was a lot of work to do. Frau Sheer had requested industrial quantities of the pathogen as soon as the results were in. Targeting genetically modified organisms to specific gene-based subgroups was the cutting edge of 21st century cellular level medicine. But he'd achieved it. From this day on Europe could be inoculated against the flood of refugees infesting every city and town and village with ox stubborn, violent stupidity.

Mother nature, with his gentle nudging, would do the clean-up work. And this time the solution would be final.

2

Sean Ryan read the headline on his news app - *Beer Hall Terrorist Caught*. It was a relief that the madman who'd shot up a beer hall in Munich a week before had been arrested, but the image he'd seen of body bags being lined up, would not be easily forgotten.

German patience was being tested, again. The bomb at the train station in Hamburg earlier that month, would have been enough to have some countries threatening retaliation on a grand scale.

He put his scuffed black leather bag on the tightly tucked-in orange bedspread. There was a musty smell in the room, as if it had been unused for a long time. He pushed open the window onto Augustiner Strasse, looked down at the passing cars and pedestrians and took a breath of cool spring air. Had he made a mistake in his choice of hotel? He'd picked it because it was within easy walking distance of the following day's conference.

No, he wasn't going to judge it on first impressions. He was going to relax. No funny smell or orange headboard or headline about the turmoil in Germany was going to stop him.

It was Friday, March 29th, the end of another busy week. The taxi from the airport had brought him into Nuremberg city centre quicker than he'd expected. That gave him more time to enjoy the city.

He unpacked, went into the bathroom. The shower head offered a multitude of settings. As he experimented with it, the water sluicing over his body, he heard his mobile ring.

The call had gone to voicemail by the time he got to it. He played back the message as he dried himself. The voice belonged to Dr Beresford-Ellis, his boss at the Institute of Applied Research in Oxford.

"Sean, when you get this, text me immediately. I need to know if you'll be at the management meeting Tuesday afternoon. As you well know, we'll be deciding on whether to take the investment we all discussed last month. Your presence would be beneficial, even if you don't agree with everything that we're planning."

Sean sat on the bed, naked. He sent a response. I'LL BE THERE. Dr Beresford-Ellis' plan for the institute was the most stupid thing he'd heard about in a long time. He was probably hoping Sean's weekend away meant he wouldn't be able to attend the meeting, but there was no way he was going to miss it.

The meeting could be his best chance to shoot the whole stinking plan down. If no one stood up to the idiot, everything the Institute had achieved would be lost within a few months. Even if he had to walk back from Nuremberg on his hands, he'd be there.

He looked at the hotel restaurant menu on a laminated card on his bedside table. He read the first few items under each heading then put it down.

The hotel claimed the restaurant was one of the best in the city, but he wanted to have a look around the old town, the Altstadt. The famous Nuremberg Christkindlesmarkt was held in the market square in front of the Frauenkirche, the Church of Our Lady, infamous as the place where Hitler held his most important early rallies. Sean couldn't resist seeing what the church and square were like, if there were still echoes of the Nazi era. He dressed quickly.

As he walked past busy shops and restaurants, he wondered how it had happened that Nuremberg became the city where millions of Germans had committed their lives to a cult that had drenched most of Europe in blood in the previous century.

At the far end of the market square there were a few stalls open under canvas and plastic canopies. As he walked across to them, the chink of glasses and the buzz of conversations drifted from restaurants at the edge of the square.

He shivered under an arctic breeze that blew across the cobblestones, then turned to walk back, heading to an Italian restaurant he'd seen. As he did, a shout rang out from a lane to his right. The lane was blocked at its far end by a tall steel-mesh barrier.

He stopped and stared down the lane. Half way down it, three shaven-headed neo-Nazi types were pushing a young couple around, jabbing at them with their hands. Then the boy was grabbed in a headlock by one of the skinheads. Sean's chest and stomach tightened.

He walked fast towards the fight.

One of the attackers was six foot of bulging muscles. The other two were shorter, but stocky. Their victims were a small Arab-looking boy in glasses and a young blond woman.

He entered the lane and his thoughts speed up. Was he being stupid? Maybe he should just report what was happening, leave it to the police?

The boy fell to the ground. The girl screamed.

The smaller of the boy's tormentors launched a kick towards the boy's head. It connected with a crunch that echoed off the high brick walls around them. The other two attackers were circling now, laughing and taunting.

Sean had no choice.

He approached the tormentors, his pulse beating hard in his neck. They had their backs to him. He did the only thing he could think of.

"Stop!" he shouted. How they'd react to someone shouting at them in English, with an American accent, he didn't care.

The larger of the attackers turned, a knife suddenly visible in his hand. His grin leered fearlessly. Sean charged straight into his shoulder, elbow first, expecting to knock the thug over. The grins on the faces of the other two thugs disappeared as he connected.

3

The fluorescent light in the records examination room blinked. The Military Archives centre in Freiburg, fifty-four miles south of Strasbourg, a bone-white office building, was like a dozen others in that corner of Germany, nestled between France and Switzerland.

The tall African woman continued fingering through the files in the long box in front of her. She wore the typical office worker uniform of black skirt and matching jacket, and her hair was tied up in a tight bun. There were over two thousand yellowing Nazi party membership cards in the box. She'd looked through most of them. They were stored alphabetically, not one out of place. So far, she had found only two with the word *Priester,* priest in German, on them, where occupation was mentioned.

The door on the far side of the room opened and a small, rotund man with breath that smelled of coffee and pastries entered.

"I am sorry," he said, stepping close to her. "There appears to be some problem with your letter of introduction." A frown creased his forehead.

The African woman looked up at him, smiled. She leaned forward, giving him another glimpse down her shirt to the light brown globes of her breasts.

"A problem?" Her German was good, but her accent was clearly foreign. She put her hand on her thigh, felt for where the thin blade was strapped to the inside of her leg.

He wouldn't be able to see her moving the hem upwards, so that she could slip the knife out.

"My colleague is having difficulty contacting the director of the archive centre, who signed your letter. He is not answering his phone."

She smiled, shook her head, as if it baffled her too. A memory of how she'd left him, naked and hanging from the bannisters of his house with a large orange in his mouth, made her smile. The morphine she'd given him wouldn't wear off for another few hours. It would take him that long again to free himself from her knots. He wouldn't be answering his phone any time soon either. And as he lived alone, interruptions to his enjoyment of the game he'd been a willing participant in were unlikely. And if they did come, it was extremely unlikely he'd ever tell anyone how he'd ended up that way.

The official looked at the sheet of paper he was holding.

"Just a very small matter, Fraulein."

She looked back down at the table. She only needed ten more minutes to look through the rest of these records. She glanced at the door. The corridor outside was quiet. No one had come down it in the hour she'd been there.

If something had gone wrong, her blade could go in between his ribs. She could lock the door behind her as soon as his heart stopped beating. That would give her enough time to get to the motorway south, the E35, and be half way to Basel before the alarm was sounded. He looked like the type who would squeal like a panicked piglet when it happened too, not even shout.

"There is no date on the director's letter. I need a date for the records." He licked his lips.

She smiled. "But he signed it for me yesterday."

"Danke," he said, as he exited the room.

Perhaps he would be back. Perhaps he had sensed something. She would have to finish quickly. She bent over the box again.

4

The older skinhead reacted with a snarl that a Rottweiler would have been proud of. He spun and lunged at Sean with his knife. The other two jeered.

"Auslander raus!" they shouted. From their mocking tone they clearly expected the confrontation to be one-sided and short.

Sean sucked in air, twisted away. He stepped back from another knife swing. Sweat popped on his forehead. His skin tingled all over, as if he already felt the cut that was coming.

With another shout the older skinhead came straight at him, the knife swinging fast from side to side. Sean grabbed for the man's wrist, gripped it, but it slipped away.

A jarring thud landed below Sean's left ear. He blinked away the shock as pain exploded across his jaw.

The shouts around him, the playground taunts, grew dim. He stumbled back. A skinhead to the side launched a huge boot encrusted foot towards him. Before he went down Sean grabbed for it. It changed course. Its tip connected with his side.

Ignoring the pain, he swung around wildly, fists pumping fast. He connected. The contact sent a judder up his arm. The larger of the thugs groaned, stepped back. Sean followed. Hit him again, in the nose. Bone and cartilage crunched beneath his knuckles.

A whistle sounded. Just as suddenly as the fight had started, it was over. Backing away fast, the three skinheads disappeared through a gap in the mesh at the end of the lane.

He looked around. Two police officers in light brown uniforms with white peaked caps firmly on their heads were running towards them. Behind them was a shiny white police car with a green stripe, its blue light flashing fast.

His jaw ached and for a moment his knees wanted to give way. He leaned against the wall of the building beside him. The girl was cradling her boyfriend's head. She turned to Sean.

"Danke, danke," she said. She was crying, her voice trembling as sobs cut through.

The police came towards them with their batons up. One of them, in a whirl of action, pushed Sean up hard against the wall, the baton across his throat. The back of Sean's head banged into the brick sending a shot of pain through his skull.

"Heh!" he shouted.

The girl was screaming at them in German. Someone else was too.

He twisted his head. An older woman was coming up the lane, a stout German woman, with short blond hair, tough looking. She was roaring at the police.

Seconds later the policeman let him go. Another police car had turned up. Its siren was blaring. The first officer shouted at him in German. Sean didn't understand the words, but the message, for him not to go anywhere was clear from the man's hand movements, pointing firmly down at the ground. The officer called the older woman over with gestures and began talking to her.

A half minute later, as Sean's heaving chest began to calm, and the pain in his jaw was fading, a female officer appeared. She asked him some questions in English. As she spoke Sean checked himself for blood. He couldn't see any. He put his hands up in front of him. The knuckles on his right hand were scratched and swollen. He bent his fingers. Thankfully nothing seemed broken.

Pointing at his hand, she said, "You must go to the hospital."

Sean took a step to the right, looked at his reflection in a shop window. There was no blood anywhere. Not that he could see. He opened his jaw. It worked. He felt his arms and legs again, felt his side, twisted his body, slowly. Nothing broken. He'd have a headache, a few other aches, but he didn't need a hospital.

"I'm okay," he said. "Thanks for turning up. Your timing was perfect."

He raised his hands. They were still shaking. He pressed them to his chest. His knuckles throbbed, but it seemed as if there would be no lasting injuries. He'd been lucky. He could have been killed. He took a deep breath, let it out slowly.

"It is better if you go to the hospital."

The police woman spoke into her mobile phone, a clunky official-looking one. The blond girl came up to Sean. Her boyfriend was clutching his side, and was on his feet behind her talking fast to a policeman, gesticulating as he spoke.

In the distance the wail of an ambulance grew louder.

"Danke, danke," said the girl again. She smiled at Sean.

"Are either of you injured?" said Sean.

She put a hand on his arm, shook her head. The boy looked towards Sean.

"You saved us," she said.

"No, I didn't. The police did that. They saved us all."

"No, no, you saved us. They would have killed us both." Her eyes were brimming.

"A Syrian student died here last week," she continued, in a rush.

Then she hugged him, tight, her breath hot in his ear for a few seconds before she stepped away.

The policewoman tapped Sean on the shoulder. She was asking more questions. The words echoed in his mind. It took a while for all the answers to come.

He gave her his name, showed his passport and the hotel room card. He turned around, to show her he had no obvious injuries.

She handed everything back to him. "You can go, sir, but our recommendation, even if you feel well, is that you visit a hospital," she said in a blunt, no-nonsense tone. "We will find you if we need a statement."

In the restaurant, half an hour later, he put his fork down after a few mouthfuls of spaghetti. It tasted rubbery. He couldn't eat. He was about to text Isabel to tell her what had happened when he stopped himself. After everything that had gone on in the past few years, it was probably a good idea if he kept his little run-in with the skinheads quiet.

He examined his face in the mirror of the restaurant bathroom. There were scratches below his ear, but it could have been worse. The bruises wouldn't be gone by Monday, but he could tell Isabel what happened then. In person. At least she wouldn't be worrying about him all weekend. She had enough to worry about. As he exited the restaurant he noticed a sticker on a lamp post outside. It was circular, about six inches wide, with - *Dritten Mal Glück* – written in old Germanic style font written on it. Behind the text was a faded white skull. It was the sort of thing you'd find on the cover of a punk band's latest website.

He stared at it. The skull reminded him of something.

5

The restaurant in the new British Library on Euston Road was not the most private of places to have a meeting. The high-ceilinged, modern, white-walled space was utilitarian, open plan. Its tables offered little protection from the gaze of onlookers.

But there was one good thing about it. The buzz of conversation in the final minutes before it closed at six that Friday evening gave Isabel the opportunity to speak to the man she had come to meet, without being overheard. She knew to meet InfoFreed contacts only in a public place. She didn't need any one telling her about basic self-protection tactics, though she appreciated Sean's concern for her security when he did ask questions about her meetings.

She couldn't stop him being obsessed with her and Alek's security, even if she wanted to. Recently, he'd even visited the home of the childminder they used now, where Alek, their son, was at that moment, to check up on the woman.

She felt an odd sensation at the back of her head. Someone was watching her. She turned quickly, didn't see anyone staring at her. Was she being over sensitive, simply because she was meeting someone she didn't know, as he claimed he had information to leak?

This wasn't going to be Edward Snowden turning up, but she still had to be careful.

The two other people she'd met so far, in similar circumstances, since she'd taken the position at InfoFreed, were friends of friends she'd felt an obligation to talk to. Another possible whistle blower, who'd contacted her, she'd referred to the InfoFreed office on Oxford Street, for one of her colleagues to deal with.

But this invitation, to meet Fred Corbett, had been impossible to turn down. So now, here she was, twisting her head slowly, wondering where Fred was. She was about to look behind her again, when a voice called out.

"Don't get up". The voice was weak.

Isabel looked around. The man standing behind her was in his eighties, at least. He had a gray moustache, thin gray hair, and translucent skin. Purple veins threaded through it, like a map drawn on his cheeks. But he had an upright, military air, and the hand that shook Isabel's was surprisingly firm.

"I saw you coming in," he said. "I just waited to be sure there was no one following you."

"Why would someone be following me?" said Isabel, looking around, as Fred sat down.

He moved closer to her as he replied. His eyes had the intensity of a man half his age, and his lips were pursed. Isabel caught a musky whiff of a strong, old-fashioned after shave.

"We don't have much time, Mrs Ryan." He gripped the edge of the table. "As I said in my email, I am here because of your grandfather." He smiled just a little. His teeth were yellow.

Isabel bit her lip. It was the first time someone had used her grandfather, James Sharpe, to arrange a meeting. She wasn't sure how to react.

"Did you know my grandfather?"

Fred licked his lips. "In 1947 I drove Major James Sharpe to the Palace of Justice in Nuremberg every morning, for six weeks. Then I was transferred to Paris." He straightened himself in his seat, coming to attention. "I've lived in France, on and off, ever since."

He paused, as if expecting her to comment. When she didn't he continued. "My parents died in the Blitz, in September, 1940."

Isabel did a quick calculation. He had to be in his early nineties.

"You must have been very young then."

"I was. I was eighteen when I met your grandfather in Nuremberg."

An odd sensation, like travelling back in time, came over Isabel. She imagined a younger Fred, what he might have looked like. The chatter of the restaurant around her diminished. Not even her own father had known Major James Sharpe. He had died soon after the war, and her father, being a young child at the time, had no memories of him.

"What was my grandfather like?"

Fred straightened himself in his seat. His knuckles protruded, ivory-white and bony, against the edge of the table.

"Do you have any idea what your grandfather's job was in Nuremberg, my dear?" He seemed agitated, his eyes darting.

"No, not really. He was on protection duties or something." She looked down. She'd never pressed her father on the details. He'd never seemed happy talking about the war and its aftermath.

"You are right, my dear, but do you know who he was protecting?" He stopped.

"No."

He shook his head sadly. "You were told how he died?" He paused, opened his mouth. It seemed as if he would cough, but then he licked his lips slowly, with a large and very pink tongue.

"I know he killed himself."

Her words came out slowly. It had been a painful fact she'd pushed out of her mind for a long time. Thinking about it brought up unwanted feelings, mostly of aching helplessness. They made something dark open up inside her, as she wondered if suicide could run in a family.

He stared at her. His eyes were pink rimmed. "I was reading about InfoFreed. You want the real truth about wrongdoing to come out, without damaging the people who leak such truths. Is that right?" His lips pressed together.

"Yes."

"Has that ever happened?"

"Has what happened?"

"That the people who leak something don't get damaged."

She thought back over the cases she'd worked on in the few months she'd been with InfoFreed.

"Why don't you tell me whatever it is you came to tell me?"

He stared at her for a good half minute before answering. She kept her expression neutral, but anticipation tensed inside her.

"Your grandfather was a good man. What happened to him was wrong, terribly wrong." A troubled look passed across her face.

"Do you know why he shot himself?" he said, softly.

A vein pulsed in her neck. A warm flush passed through her.

"I heard he was affected by what he saw at Nuremberg." She looked down at the table, then away across the room at the diners chatting, oblivious, cheerful. "That's all I was told. That it was something to do with the trials."

"You know they were fixed, don't you?"

"What do you mean?" She stared into his eyes. He'd have to come up with some pretty strong evidence before she swallowed that theory.

"Are you a practicing Catholic, Mrs Ryan?"

It was a long time since someone had asked her about her religion. She shrugged.

"My father was, but he lapsed. I never took to any of it, despite being sent to a Catholic school. So the answer is no, I'm not."

"I see." His eyes widened.

For a moment Isabel wondered if she was dealing with someone who was mentally damaged.

"Do you know why Hitler attacked Russia and lost the war, Mrs Ryan?"

She didn't reply.

"You do know that if he'd kept to his treaty with Stalin, the Normandy landings would have failed, or never have happened?"

She shrugged. She hadn't thought about such a question since she was in school.

"Didn't he attack Russia because he was running out of oil?"

Fred shook his head.

"No." He put a purple veined finger in the air between them. "That is not the reason. That's what they tell us the reason is." He glanced over her shoulder.

Isabel twisted in her seat. The old woman at the table behind them was staring openly at her.

"Is that your wife?"

Fred nodded. "She doesn't approve of me talking to you."

"Why?"

He leaned closer, so close she could smell his breath, a faint toothpasty smell, warm on her hands in front of her.

"She thinks I should have destroyed everything I have a long time ago."

"What do you have?"

"Come to our hotel. I'll show you." He waved at his wife. "It will be worth it, I promise you."

"I'm not sure."

Even if he did have some information relating to the war, she wasn't at all sure if she should go with him. It was better to do these sorts of things in public.

He reached into his inside pocket, pulled out a note written on yellow hotel paper. He handed it to Isabel. There were two sentences on it, and a signature. *When the time is right, please make sure what we spoke about reaches the public. In the name of all that is dear to us.*

Underneath was a scrawled *Major James Sharpe*. The date, December 12, 1947, was beside the signature.

It had been written the month before her grandfather had died. She remembered her father's drinking binges each January. An image of circles closing came to her. Her fingers trembled. She passed him back the note.

"We could meet again tomorrow." She shouldn't accept being rushed.

"My wife asked a priest what we should do, about what I want to show you, before we die." Both his hands came up. They shook in front of her. "Since then we've received odd telephone calls. Strange men have turned up at our apartment block in Paris." He threw his hands in the air.

"But who would care now why Hitler attacked Russia?" He shook his head. "If you were Russian, Mrs. Ryan, a relative of one of the twenty million who died in the Second World War perhaps, you would not say that. There's a lot of interest in such things these days, as the Soviet archives are finally opened."

"Why don't you hand over what you have to the authorities?"

He shook his head. "If the authorities get hold of what I have, it will be suppressed or destroyed. Every last atom." He was agitated again. "Your grandfather's wish will not be fulfilled. The truth will never come out. The truth about why your grandfather died. And why so many millions died in that terrible war. Many of the people who enabled all those deaths have never been prosecuted, never mind punished, Mrs Ryan!"

"So this is the right time for everything to come out?" She was thinking about what her grandfather had said in his note.

"Yes, society has changed. People question things now. They are more open to the truth." He leaned toward her. "There are other reasons too. If you come, I will tell you."

The thought of making one of her grandfather's wishes come true was hard to resist. She had to make a decision.

"I have to make a call first." Her voice was firm. "If our childminder can take our son for another few hours, I'll go with you."

Fred was shaking his head.

"You must come, Mrs Ryan." He held his hand out to her. It was jerking, as if he was ill.

Isabel had her phone to her ear. She smiled at him.

It was a few minutes before her call finished. By that time Fred's wife was sitting beside him. She was talking in French to her husband.

6

Sean was back in his hotel within two hours of the incident in the lane. A quick visit to the bar and a large shot of whiskey had steadied his hands. A dull thumping in his jaw and in his side told him he'd had enough fun for one night.

The following morning, he had breakfast in the Spartan hotel restaurant. As he watched a harried husband taking a plate of eggs and cheese slices to his much larger wife, he remembered the fundamental truth about German life, which had been taught to him one night by a colleague at the institute, who was from Hamburg.

"Schiller is our God. Obedience the first duty. That was his number one saying. If you want to understand us Germans, understand that." He'd leaned towards Sean as he'd said it, as if he'd just imparted something profound.

"Which is why I love Oxford," he'd continued. "I am free to bend the rules here, with only consequences as my guide." He'd beamed at Sean then.

He could even remember the man's perfect teeth as he'd smiled.

Sean put his fork in his mouth. One thing he couldn't argue with was the quality of Nuremberg sausage.

He headed for the reception desk as soon as he was finished. He'd arranged to meet a professor of modern history, Eleni Kibre, from the Free University of Nuremberg, at nine thirty. It was exactly that time when she walked into the small, but gleaming reception area.

"Sean Ryan! It's a wonderful blessing to see you," said Eleni. They hugged. The coolness of the Germanic way of life hadn't taken away one little bit of her Zambian warmth. They hugged for at least thirty seconds. They'd dated when Sean was in college in London. His memory of her was of a sensuous, fun-loving woman who'd disappeared back home to Lusaka when her conservative Christian family had found out that she was staying over in his room almost every weekend.

Now she was an academic rock star, the only African professor of modern history in Germany. She had controversial ideas, too. She argued them well in the German media, as well as through academic papers. Too well in some people's view.

They'd met again at a conference in Cambridge the previous summer. Sean had invited her and her partner to meet Isabel in London.

"How is that wonderful wife of yours, and your beautiful son?" were Eleni's first words after she'd hugged him.

"All good."

She kept hold of his wrists, pulled away and looked hard into his eyes.

"You've put that beautiful family of yours through a lot."

Her smile widened playfully. Eleni was one of the main reasons he'd agreed to attend the award ceremony and conference in Nuremberg. He looked forward to seeing her, to experiencing her light hearted free spirit.

"How's your book on the dark side of human behavior going?" she asked.

"Slowly," he replied.

They talked all the way to the car park. She stopped at a battered green BMW. It was the oldest car in the area.

"I get people staring at me all the time in this." She laughed. "But we'll get to our destination in fifteen minutes, exactly the same time as if I had a sparkling new Mercedes." She buckled her seat belt. "Come on, tell me everything that has been happening at the institute. I want to know all the dirty little secrets. Who is sleeping with who?" Her gaze flickering toward him as she moved the car out of its space.

"Nobody's sleeping with anyone right now, Eleni. Not that I know. But I'm always the last to find out about those things."

"You disappoint me. I was hoping for some juicy gossip," said Eleni.

They talked about old times as they passed under a bridge and across railroad tracks, and trundled over tram tracks.

After twenty minutes she pulled into a parking space near the front of the giant former Congress Hall of the Nazi party, the place where the Nuremberg rallies had been held. The building was surrounded by a ring of tall plane trees. They lined the nearby streets and stretched away far into the distance.

The Congress Hall reminded Sean of the Colosseum in Rome, but this was a concrete version, with three tiered archway levels, one above the other, each smaller than the one below. The building was curved, as if it would form a circle, though only half the circle had been constructed. Whatever the plan had been, the building must have been capable of holding tens of thousands of spectators.

"It's incredible, isn't it," said Eleni, as they got out and looked up.

"There are seven square miles of rally grounds here," said Eleni. "Those Nazi's knew how to manage big events."

"Can visitors go inside?" said Sean.

Eleni pointed to the left. "There's a visitor center over there, but that's not what we're here for. I promised you a visit to something the public never gets to see, and I never break my promises. You know that." She nudged him and winked.

They walked under the trees, heading for the cliff face of the Congress Hall looming above them. The concrete colour matched the dark gray lid of clouds that filled the sky. The smell of something burning hung in the air.

The lower level of the building was a slightly lighter shade of concrete than the ones above. Green steel doors circled the building at ground level, about twenty feet apart. Above ground level there was a railing and a set of tall arches, embedded into and circling the building.

The door they stopped in front of had the words - *Eintritt verboten* – in red letters printed on it.

"Are you sure we're allowed to go in?" said Sean.

"Don't worry," said Eleni. "Everything is forbidden in Germany, unless you have permission." She tapped the small, black leather bag tucked under her arm. "I have permission in writing to visit this and some other interesting sites I can tell you about."

Inside the door was a long bare corridor lit by a window high above the door they had just come through. Eleni put a hand to a bulky yellow light switch. Lights flickered on above their heads.

"This passage runs to the center of the building, right below where the main stage would have been. It was a quick way for speakers to get in and out."

They walked down the corridor, their footsteps echoing into the distance. Sean asked Eleni how they were treating her at the university.

"The admin staff are wonderful, really, but I hate it there these days," she whispered, leaning towards him. "Some of the new students make my skin crawl. You'd be shocked if I told you what I've had to listen to."

7

I shouldn't be here. I shouldn't be breathing. I should be dust.

He stared out of the window. A group of old women were talking in the cobbled square below, but he wasn't looking at them. He was seeing something else. Something from a nightmare.

A nightmare as clear as any memory. Skeletons were walking toward him. Bony faces with eyes so sunken he could see the oval sockets. Each mouth was open. Blood dripped from their lips, achingly slowly, dropping from chins onto chests, splattered red already.

Voices, a shrieking jangle of words he couldn't understand, echoed through his mind, rising and falling. An ancient smell, a stinking odor of shit and blood and sweat, twitched at his nostrils. He closed his eyes tight, crinkling his face. The skeletons were still there. He shook his head, tried to rise, to get away, but his legs wouldn't work.

They hadn't worked in a long time. How long was it since they'd been strong?

He couldn't remember. He raised his right hand, high, made it into a fist, held it in front of his face. It shook. The paper-thin skin barely covered his bones. His knuckles protruded like broken stones. He pushed his hand out, fast, then pulled it back, striking his forehead as hard as he could. The crack of bones connecting echoed in the empty day room. He blinked, salty tears forming. His arm trembled and jerked, as he placed it down on his lap.

Then his head went back until it met the plastic of the high-backed chair. The throb in his forehead was all he could think about now. It sent snaking tendrils of pain down his neck and across his chin. But the faces were gone. The voices had faded.

The clatter of a trolley coming into the day room startled him. He turned his head, his mouth wide open.

When he saw the pale green smock of the kitchen assistant with the white emblem of hands held together above a heart, he remembered where he was, the Kreigeshof Old People's home in the Aldstat of Nuremberg. He'd been here a long time.

He held a hand out. The girl with the trolley was new. She was pretty, too, tall, African. He smiled. Perhaps she would hold him, like the other one used to, long ago. Something stirred in his groin, as he examined the shape of her legs under her uniform. He leaned forward. This would be a good day.

His smile widened.

Then he saw what was in her hand. What was she going to use that for?

8

Sean smiled. He'd remembered how Eleni used to complain about the students in her class when he'd dated her.

"The refugee situation can't be helping."

"It's not the refugees I worry about, Sean. It's the changing attitudes of Germans. There's a pack of students who go around shouting at anyone who doesn't look German enough for them."

"They shout at you?"

"Yes. Things I'll never repeat. It makes me sick. You don't have any jobs going at the institute, do you?"

"Sorry," he said. "We have a freeze on hiring." It was his ready answer to any questions about jobs. The institute had no hope of taking on all the well qualified people who wanted to work there.

They exited the passage into a circular underground hall. Its age-blackened concrete roof was fifteen feet above them.

"I believe Adolf initiated his friends here." Eleni turned, shook her head. "That must have been a sight."

"Unusual decorations," said Sean. He pointed at the circle of red brick walls around them. Stylised animal shapes stood out in different shades of red and cream bricks.

"Yes."

She went to the centre of the room and stepped onto a slightly raised brick area. She held her hands out, palms outstretched.

"Tell me if you feel anything." She closed her eyes and recited.

"Exorcizamus te, omnis immundus spiritus." Then she turned, forty-five degrees, and repeated the phrase.

"What the hell is that supposed to do?" said Sean.

"Ssshhh," said Eleni. She turned again, repeated the phrase, then did it all one more time.

Sean waited. "It's getting cold," he said. "Are we going for lunch?"

"I thought you'd never ask." Eleni stepped down from the raised area.

"Have a look at these bricks before we go." She pointed at where she'd been standing.

"What was that you just recited?"

"An exorcism chant."

"Appropriate."

Sean was standing on the square of red bricks, looking down. There were faded white lines painted on it in the shape of an arrow, with a Swastika above it. He shivered, despite his leather jacket.

"It's cold down here."

She stood in front of him. "I wanted you to see this, after that last email of yours."

He peered closer at the lines.

"Do you know how Herr Hitler came to power?"

"He was elected, right? Democracy in action."

"Actually, the Nazi party needed other parties to gain total power. The Catholic Zentrum party tipped the balance at the moment he needed it in the German parliament in 1933."

"Bad call, right."

"It was more than that, Sean. The Vatican gave crucial support to Adolf internationally. Four months after the Nazi party took full power, the Vatican signed the first foreign treaty with Hitler's regime, giving his dictatorship the international recognition it badly needed."

"That's what friends are for."

She held his arm, her voice dropping to a whisper as she continued.

"Exorcizamus te, omnis immundus spiritus," she whispered.

"Now you're spooking me."

She let go of him. "Come on. I know a restaurant that makes proper pasta. You still like pasta, don't you?"

A queue of cars was leaving the underground car park in the old city when they arrived back. None were heading in.

"Where's everyone going?"

"There's a demonstration in the market square this afternoon. Most people won't want to be anywhere near it." Eleni took the ticket out of the machine and drove slowly up the circular ramp.

"What kind of a demonstration?"

"A sick one," she said. "It's a march to commemorate the Allied raid on Nuremberg in 1944. Neo-Nazis up to their old tricks again."

"I thought all the demonstrations were against Syrian refugees and the mosque building program."

"They start as one thing, then spin into another. This demonstration is organized by the National Peace Party. They claim they want peace and freedom for all Germans."

"We'll get to see this demonstration?"

"I hope not."

9

The BXH bank building in Frankfurt is within coin-tossing distance of the European Central Bank headquarters in the Kaiserplatz, the business area of the city. The glass-walled hundred-and-fifty-meter spear-shaped tower reflects the River Main, which eddies by in grey and green currents only twenty meters away.

The top of the BXH building, the head of the spear, was given over to the senior executives of BXH. One section of that floor had been fitted out in the style of a Chinese temple. Low black tables were surrounded by bamboo mats and thick cushions.

The top-floor meeting rooms were rarely used. The traditional German board room, beyond the Chinese meeting room, was the main area where business was conducted. It had a giant polished oak table with shiny aluminium and black leather chairs around it.

That Saturday afternoon, three people sat in the board room overlooking the Main River. An LCD screen, hanging from the ceiling at the end of the table by steel wires, played a feed from Nuremberg's main square, showing lines of policemen. The sound had been turned down.

Vanessa Sheer, European CEO of BXH, was speaking. She had her hands on the table in front of her, pressing down. Her thick blond hair swayed a little as she spoke. A whiff of expensive perfume drifted around her.

"When this group was established by our predecessors, including my own grandfather, they had one objective - the rebuilding of the German nation to take its rightful place as the leader of the world. We must not lose sight of that. These demonstrators are right."

She waved at the screen. "Fifty thousand people have come out to demand something is done about the rape and abuse of the women of Germany. It is a disgrace that our government has allowed this to continue, year after year. The mosque building program is absurd, too. Do you think they'd allow us build hundreds of Christian churches in Muslim countries?" She paused, leaned forward. "There can be no turning back."

Monsignor Salerna, the silver-haired representative of the Vatican Bank on the BXH board, stared at the table in front of him. When Vanessa Sheer finished speaking, he straightened himself, and brushed his hair across his high forehead.

"Monsignor," said Vanessa, turning to him. "Would you like to add your thoughts?"

She smiled at him, as she withdrew her hands from the table. Vanessa Sheer was still only forty-five, and her tight-fitting suits meant she was often mistaken for a trophy wife at the parties she attended. She rarely corrected such opinions. She took them as a compliment.

The Monsignor returned her smile for a few milliseconds longer than was necessary.

"The German public health service will have no hope of coping with what you are about to throw at them." He raised a finger, pointed at Sheer.

"I must be sure our Catholic flock will not become victims, or if they do, that the numbers will be small."

Sheer's expression was granite-like. "Let me state it clearly, then, Monsignor. The numbers of German Catholic victims should be zero. That is our goal. It has always been our goal. I have stated this over and over."

"And you are sure the right group will be blamed for what will happen in Nuremberg?"

She nodded.

The third man looked from Sheer to the Monsignor. His eyes were steel gray. This wasn't a man who agreed to anything lightly. His conglomerate of German manufacturing companies was one of the biggest in the country. He stared out the window toward the ECB tower. Then he spoke, softly.

"*Gut*. But let us do it quickly. There must be minimal economic impact, Vanessa, *verstanden*?"

Sheer nodded.

His tone softened. "We all want this refugee problem solved. We cannot have armed police at every bierkeller and bag searches at every metro station for ever."

Vanessa stood, went around the table, shook her colleagues" hands, slowly and deliberately. "This is a day to remember, gentlemen."

She smiled at the Monsignor. It elicited a light flush on the Monsignor's cheeks.

She whispered in his ear. "We will have the task you set us complete soon, Monsignor. All the evidence will disappear forever, and the witnesses, too."

The Monsignor crossed himself and nodded. Then he followed the others out of the room.

10

When Sean and Eleni arrived down at street level, after exiting the car park, it was clear something major was going on. Groups of people were heading toward the center of the old town. A watchfulness hung in the air, and people looked around nervously.

"I don't expect we'll see much. The police will only let them march to the square, then they'll have to disperse. It will all be over by the time we're finished lunch," said Eleni, as they stood aside to let a group of people pass.

The Italian restaurant they went to was closed. Two other restaurants they tried were closed as well. There were hand-written notes on the insides of the windows.

Eleni translated one.

"They've all gone home."

"We can eat at my hotel. They have to keep their restaurant open."

"Sure, but I won't stay long. All this disruption is too upsetting," Eleni replied.

The hotel restaurant was open. It was busy too, packed with residents as well as non-residents who couldn't find anywhere else to eat.

As they ate their meal they watched, along with most of the room, as the demonstration and a counter demonstration played out on an LCD TV screen high up in a far corner above a small bar. Lines of hand-holding anti-Nazi demonstrators were visible in the square. A commentator was talking fast in German.

"What's happening?" said Sean. He pushed his plate away. His pasta had been a little hard. He didn't feel like finishing it.

"Look," said Eleni. She put her knife and fork down, pointed at the screen as a group of black clad demonstrators, ten abreast, came into view.

She waved her fist at them. "Bloody Nazis," she hissed. A few people turned towards her, gave her blank looks, neither sympathetic nor condemning. Someone in the far corner made a comment in German. It did not sound like a compliment.

A murmur went up from the people in the room. On the screen a giant black man with thick dreadlocks, dressed in bright green trousers and wearing a green hoodie, had appeared. He was leading two large Alsatian dogs. A black clad policewoman was running towards him.

The man stood in front of the line of anti-immigrant demonstrators. He released his Alsatians. They reared up, leaping at two of the demonstrators, who raised their hands to protect themselves.

The policewoman reached the man and grabbed his arm. The TV commentator stopped talking. The dogs turned and ran back to their master. A scream rang out from the TV. The dogs were attacking the policewoman.

A gasp went up around them. A thick buzz of German rose in the air, as if bees had been frightened. A few people turned and stared at them. The commentator began talking again, but faster.

"I have to go," said Eleni. She sounded flustered.

Sean followed her. He sensed she was upset at what she'd just witnessed. He offered to walk to her car with her.

"Did I miss something back there?" he said, as they walked. The streets had a deserted feel.

Eleni walked fast. "It's the mood here, Sean. It's changed. I'm frightened. I can feel it here, inside." She pressed a hand to her chest. "When the people around me don't approve of my presence." She sounded hurt, on the verge of tears.

"Eleni, you're being paranoid."

"I am not being paranoid. Look at that." She pointed at a street light they were passing.

For a few seconds Sean wasn't sure what she meant. Then he saw the sticker with the words *Dritten Mal Glück* on it.

"What the hell does that mean? It looks like something to do with a rock band,"

"It's not a rock band," she said. "*Dritten Mal Glück* means third time lucky. It's a bunch of fascists making a statement about the world wars. You know, next time we win. They have a sick website people can sign up for."

"We get fascist stuff in London sometimes too. I wouldn't worry about it. There's idiots everywhere."

"It's different when you're the target, Sean. I hate it. I hate it all." There was bitterness in her voice. She glanced around, her eyes wide.

"Don't let them get to you."

"Come to our apartment," she said. "You'll see what's going on."

They'd reached the door to the stairs that led up to where Eleni had parked her car. They turned to each other.

"Jerome will be there. He'd love to meet you. I want you to understand why I'm like this."

They reached her apartment at one forty-five. Later, Sean remembered this, because he checked his phone for messages and saw the clock on the screen. The apartment was in a six-storey building on a road with a tramway down the centre and electric cables running above the street like steel cobwebs.

Her building had a small book store on the ground floor. There was a park with a children's playground and metal climbing frames across the street. The playground was empty. The street was clean, but it had a deserted feel. "Everybody's inside, watching the demonstration. They say it will be the largest in Nuremberg in fifty years," said Eleni, as they walked around from the car park at the back of the building.

As they came to the front door Sean saw there were two stickers with *Dritten Mal Glück* on them on the thick aluminium pole outside her front door. They were similar to the stickers in the centre of the city, but these were red.

Eleni scraped at them with her nails, almost frantically. Her reaction took Sean completely by surprise.

"I knew they'd be here again. I hate them. I hate them watching us." She turned to him, her face pale. "They don't like foreigners in their precious Nuremberg." Her scratching had removed only part of one sticker. She went back to attacking the rest of it.

11

The old man stared at the thin steel blade. A memory rose, unbidden, of a similar knife, one he'd owned once, a long time ago. A shiver ran through him.

"What?" His High German accent still remained, but his tone was mild, pleading.

"Where did you hide the letters?" said the African girl. She moved the knife close to his stomach.

"Answer me, old man."

It had been a long time since anyone had threatened him. His mind fogged. What was she asking him about? A vague memory of something important struggled to come to the surface.

He opened his mouth, summoned a breath.

A rubber-gloved hand clamped tight over his lips.

"Fifteen, fourteen, thirteen, twelve . . ." She pushed the point of the blade up to the front of his old gray shirt.

"It can take up to an hour to die, if your guts are spilled out, but I am sure you know that. There will be no way they can fix you. Answer me or die screaming."

"Uggghh," he struggled to speak. She took her hand away.

"Catherine's," he whispered. A glint of hope filled his eyes.

The hand clamped hard again. He bit, tried to swing his head from side to side, but he hadn't much strength left, and her grip was too hard. He grunted, as she smiled at him. His hands were on her arms now, but they had no power.

A thick wet torrent fell on his knees. His eyes opened wide. She pulled something wet and warm and pressed it into his left hand.

His face twisted in pain. His insides spilled.

She was beside his ear now.

"Thank you. I will lock the door and leave you here in torment, Father Zegliwski. It is what you deserve." She stepped back.

He spat towards her with the last of his spittle.

She reached to the trolley, took one of the kitchen knives and pressed the point of it into his stomach, causing another spasm of searing pain to run like a hot knife through his body. Then she pressed the knife into his right hand and closed his grip on the handle.

"You did the right thing, old man," she said. Then she pushed the trolley out of the day room.

12

Sean scratched at the other sticker with a coin.

A couple went past them. The woman made a tutting noise, disapproving of something. Sean turned to her, but she didn't look back. Whether she had been disapproving of the stickers, or of Eleni and Sean trying to remove them was unclear.

"This is crazy," he said. "You mean these things keep coming back, even after you rip them off?"

"Crazy is only a little piece of it. You try living here. You'd go stark raving mad." She got the last section of her sticker off, as Sean peeled a big piece away from his.

"Leave the rest. Come up. Jerome should be here. He's from Rwanda. You'll like him."

They took a small elevator. It rattled as it went up. Jerome was holding the door open when they reached her apartment. His red and yellow shirt hung loose outside his trousers. It had a giant picture of Nelson Mandela on its front. From behind him thumping African music reverberated into the corridor.

Eleni smiled shyly, as she put her arm around her boyfriend's waist.

This is Jerome. He teaches at the university."

"I'm a professor of genetics." Jerome smiled. On the wall behind him a double helix strand had been turned into a painting.

"Turn down that music and bring Sean inside," said Eleni.

Jerome shook Sean's hand, then led him into the main room of the apartment.

"Heh, you didn't go out?" said Eleni, when she joined them with a steaming pot of coffee and some red and yellow mugs on a tray a few minutes later.

"I've been watching the demonstration. Did you see it?" Jerome, turned to Sean. His lips were pressed together and his eyes had widened.

"We saw some of it on TV. I'd no idea it was this bad here."

"Something's happened," said Jerome. "This is the worst I've ever seen it. They're even covering it on CNN. It's at the Frauenkirche." He pointed a remote control at the small TV screen on a table in the corner of the room. Wooden African masks and a red tapestry filled the wall behind the TV.

The channel changed to CNN, the English version. They were covering the aftermath of the demonstration, replaying scenes of people running.

"The demonstration is over, isn't it?" said Eleni.

"I don't know, there's been arrests," said Jerome. "Some *dick kopf* attacked the march with his dogs. Windows were smashed. It brings back too many memories." He looked at Eleni, shook his head, mouthed something, as if he was continuing some other conversation he'd been having with her.

"I saw the stickers," said Sean.

Jerome grabbed Sean's shoulder, squeezed it.

"Maybe you can get Eleni to see sense. We have to move. We have to. I saw all this back home, in Kigali. They mark the houses when they're going to kill people. Then they come for you." He drew his hand across his throat.

Eleni patted his back. He swung his arm around, pushed her away, hard.

She backed up.

"Calm down, there isn't a civil war here, Jerome," she said. "This is Germany. No one's going around killing people because of what tribe they're in."

He shook his head, fast. "You heard that, Sean. She won't listen to me. Stubbornness, that's what you call it in English, isn't it?" He reached out, his fist tight. "Many people were murdered in this city because of who they were. You know some researchers are digging up the Frauenkirche! I expect they'll find a lot of bodies under it. Those demonstrators probably went there to stop it!"

"Pogroms don't happen any more," said Eleni.

"No?" said Jerome. "But they've been arresting refugees. Did you know that? Last night a boy was arrested in the market square. He'd been attacked by these thugs." He gestured at the TV. "He was arrested. A friend at the University told me about it. The police only released the boy this morning. Who will they come for next?"

"I intervened in a fight in the old town last night," said Sean. He told them everything that had happened.

Jerome shook his hand. "You did good, my friend. You do know you were lucky?" He turned to Eleni. "We mightn't be so lucky. We must leave this apartment soon as we can. Please, let's go, Eleni." There was desperation in his tone.

Eleni shook her head. "We have to give proper notice. We can't just up and leave. Anyway, order will be restored. Every German loves order. If we're not safe here, we're not safe anywhere in this country."

Jerome put his hands to his head, rocked back and forth. "I have a bad feeling in here," he said. He pointed at his abdomen. "It's eating at me." His hand made a fist. He pressed it deep into his stomach.

Eleni put her hand on his arm. Jerome looked sad now, his anger dissipating.

Sean changed the subject. "Tell me about this book you're working on, Eleni. Are you part of it, Jerome?"

Eleni talked about the book. Jerome just wrung his hands. He didn't get involved in the conversation. A few minutes later he went out of the room. The tension stayed though. Half an hour later Eleni offered to drive Sean back into the city.

Jerome handed Sean his business card at the door. "If you come across any jobs for a couple of itinerant academics, please email me, please." There was unsettling desperation in his voice.

Sean put the card in his wallet. "I will, if I see anything."

Jerome smiled. "Forgive me for asking." They shook hands.

When they reached the front of the building there were three red stickers on the lamp post. A tingle ran up Sean's back. These were new stickers. He looked around at the houses and shops. Had someone been watching them remove the other ones?

He felt an odd sensation, as he looked at the rows of sightless windows. Was that twitching curtain some neo-Nazi neighbour trying to frighten Eleni and Jerome away?

She waved her hand in the air. "Leave them, leave them," she said. "I'll clean them away tomorrow."

"Jerome worries me," she said, as she drove him back through the city. "He finds it hard to escape the past."

"Maybe he has a point about what's going on here."

She tutted. "We can't move. You shouldn't encourage him. I'm not going to run away." They'd stopped at traffic lights. She spoke softly.

"They cannot win, Sean. We've invested too much. Jerome is about to publish a paper on genetically matched medicine. It'll be good for his career, a major breakthrough by a Rwandan scientist. It will establish his name. We've waited too long for this. If we leave Nuremberg, he will have to leave his job. His paper won't be published. You can't walk out on a professorship in this country. It would be the end for him. All he has worked for would be wasted."

"Can you not just move to another part of town?"

"We tried that, last summer. There were stickers at our previous place too, though it wasn't as bad as this. They'd find us quickly."

"Have you gone to the police?"

She made a growling noise. "They always say they will do something, but then nothing happens." She gestured dismissively.

He felt powerless. "Maybe it's just teenagers."

They talked about the old days in college as Eleni drove on. The streets were busy again. By the time he got back to the hotel everything seemed to be back to normal. The restaurants outside on the street were open, people were strolling around.

Sean went up to his room, had a shower, then called Isabel in London. She was at home with their son. He spoke to Isabel, then to Alek for a few minutes.

Then he read his emails on his phone and ran through his speech. The awards ceremony was starting at seven. He would have to leave the hotel by six-thirty to get there on time. The ceremony was in the Free University of Nuremberg in a northern suburb of the city. His speech, about how he'd discovered an unknown mass grave near Dachau, north of Munich, thanks to satellite image analysis, was as short as he could get away with. Dachau was the first concentration camp the Nazis established. They'd used it to murder political opponents. The discovery of a new mass grave had not been universally welcomed. Trolls had attacked his Facebook page.

If his paper inspired anyone to do more research on the site, he would consider it a success. His speech was billed as a highlight of the evening, but as it was his only speaking slot at the conference he suspected he was simply a time-filler, before the awards were announced afterwards.

As he was getting ready to leave a knock sounded on his door. He looked through the viewfinder and was literally taken aback. Three German police officers were in the corridor. The officer directly in front of the door knocked again.

His muscles tensed. For a second, while he watched the men through the spy hole, he wondered if they were police at all. Maybe he shouldn't open the door? If they were only dressed up as policemen, they were certainly doing an amazing acting job. They had even got the slouching and the tight haircuts right.

"Polizei!" the voice from the other side of the door echoed though the room.

He pulled the door open.

They pushed him back with the speed of their entry.

"What the hell is this about?" he said.

"Herr Ryan, ja?" said an older officer. His hair was almost pure white, except for a touch of yellow on his fringe, which looked like a nicotine stain.

"Yes. What do you want?"

One of the other officers flicked through the two books Sean had put on the bed side table.

"We have a *Durchsuchungsbefehl*, a search warrant I believe you call it, for this room, Herr Ryan. I hope you will cooperate with us."

The third policeman, a blond, blue-eyed, thin young officer, had taken up position in front of the door out of the room and was watching Sean.

"I've nothing to hide. What the hell is this all about?"

"You recently had a shower, I see," said the older officer. He'd poked his nose in the bathroom.

"Yes, I did." He restrained himself from commenting that it wouldn't have taken Sherlock Holmes to deduce that. The mist on the mirror and the damp towel on the bed were the sort of clues a child could have followed.

"Is there a reason you are having a shower in the afternoon?"

"What? I'm going to an award ceremony this evening. That's why I'm in Nuremberg. I'm getting ready. Is that illegal?" He spoke slowly, deliberately.

"We will need to take these," said the older policeman. He was pointing at a large see-through plastic Ziploc bag, which his colleague was holding out. Inside it was the light blue shirt and the navy trousers Sean had been wearing that morning. He had put on the black suit he had brought with him for the award ceremony.

"This is freaking me out. Are you going to tell me what this is all about?" A tingle of anxiety twisted in his gut.

"All in good time, Herr Ryan. All in good time."

Sean looked at his watch. Time was something he didn't have much of.

"I have to go soon," he said. But he knew, with a sinking sensation enveloping him, that there was something serious going on, and that he'd be lucky to get away quickly.

The older, white haired policeman stopped what he was doing, looking in a bedside cupboard, and looked up at Sean.

"Herr Ryan, you will not be going anywhere soon. We are investigating a murder."

13

Isabel gripped the arm of her chair. They had arrived at the Intercontinental Hyde Park Hotel only a few minutes before, and were now in a large double room on the sixth floor, overlooking the gardens of Buckingham Palace. The armchair she was sitting on was covered in a pale blue paisley fabric. It matched the carpet, the curtains and the bedspread.

She had only agreed to come up to the room because Fred Corbett's wife, Daisy, had begged her to not to make them talk in public. She had taken Isabel's arm in the foyer and had guided her towards the elevators, while glancing from side to side and whispering about who might be watching them.

When they were settled in the room, after Fred had checked the corridor to ensure no one had followed them, he sat opposite her, on the other side of the coffee table.

"You seem a little paranoid," said Isabel.

Fred glanced at his wife before responding. "We have to be very careful," he said. "We don't want to be silenced."

"You really think someone wants to silence you?"

"I do, young lady. The truth about all the people who supported Adolf Hitler's rise to power has never been revealed."

Isabel took a long breath, sat back. "Isn't it all a matter of public record? Historians have been crawling over the Nazi archives for decades." Isabel looked from Fred to Daisy and back again. Daisy looked pale.

Fred was shaking his head.

"I am sorry, you are wrong. Most people are about all this. One archive at least is still missing. Pope Pius XII's secretary destroyed all his letters when he died in nineteen fifty-eight. Most of his correspondence with Herr Hitler is not available for anyone to study. The Vatican has only opened up part of their general archive for the period to researchers, even all these years later." He leaned across the coffee table to Isabel. His skin seemed to be pulled tight across his forehead, exposing a mesh of blue veins.

"The most incriminating material is not even in Rome."

"So, where is it?"

"We have some of it," said Fred, in a low voice. He stared at Isabel, as if daring her to argue with him.

Isabel looked around. "Don't tell me you have this evidence here, with you." She was starting to doubt her wisdom in coming up to their room. Were they both delusional?

Fred pointed at the bed.

Isabel suppressed a smile. She should have guessed they would hide something important under the mattress. Who would look there?

Daisy, who had been sitting on the third chair, the one nearest the bed, turned and slid her hand under the corner of the mattress. She pulled out an old brown envelope. Its edges were a caramel colour and its flap was folded inside the opening.

Fred took the envelope and reached inside.

"I have not shown these photographs to anyone else, but my wife, since nineteen forty-nine, when I was demobbed." As he spoke, he slid a few small yellowing photographs out of the envelope. He caressed them, as if they were alive, then passed them to Isabel. She took them carefully, her fingers holding their edge.

The prints were rectangular, about the size of her hand. There were three of them. She brought them close to her face. The first showed the back of a square envelope. The image had a large yellow seal on it and above that a blue coat of arms. She wasn't sure, but it looked like the Papal emblem on the coat of arms. It had two crossed keys in gold. The other two pictures showed the back and front of a letter. It had large, hand written script on it.

There were flourishes on every word, spirals and swirls extending above and below each line. What caught her attention though, were the words, *Reich Chancellor*, at the top of the first page and, *Pius PP XII*, written in a large hand-written style, with a single line flourish below it, which was on the bottom of the second page.

It certainly looked as if these were genuine photographs of a letter from Pope Pius XII, the pope during all of the Second World War. She moved one picture closer.

"You won't be able to read it, dear," said Daisy. "It's in German."

"The Vatican always wrote to foreign heads of state in their own language," added Fred.

Isabel put the pictures on the coffee table. "Have you translated the text?"

Fred and Daisy looked at each other. "We did a rough translation fifty years ago, but we've never had it verified," said Fred.

"Why not?"

Fred sat back, put his hand to his forehead. He opened his mouth, but he stopped and shook his head. A few seconds later Daisy spoke. Her tone was low, almost apologetic.

"In this letter the Pope encourages Hitler to defeat Communism, to confront Russia."

Daisy coughed. Fred did too.

Isabel peered at the picture. "You didn't think a lot people would be interested in this?"

Fred shrugged.

Then another thought came to her. "Did you want to protect the church?"

Daisy nodded, just slightly, but enough to make it clear that Isabel had guessed right.

"I believed in the Church for most of my life. I told Fred to burn these a long time ago." She pointed at the pictures.

"Why?"

"We were told that Communism was evil. That it wanted to enslave us all. Anything that was done to defeat it seemed a wonderful idea."

"What made you change your mind?"

"My faith has been. . ." She hesitated. "Undermined."

Fred added. "Recently we got a phone call from a priest I met in Germany a long time ago. He was a young man then, hearing confessions." He stopped, wiped a hand across his brow, then continued. "He called me from his death bed. He said he knew I had these photographs. He said he was the person who'd passed this letter to your grandfather. It was your grandfather who gave me these pictures. Before." He paused. "You know." He stopped. Isabel nodded.

"The priest told me something else, too." He looked pained.

"What?"

"He said there are other letters. Letters like this one. He said we he had a duty to reveal their existence, no matter what the consequences."

"Why would a priest want to undermine his own church?" It didn't sound believable.

Fred stared at her, his expression solemn. "He said there are plans." He stopped, looked her in the eye. "For a new holocaust."

"A new holocaust? What the hell?" She wondered again whether to take any of this seriously.

"I asked him to tell me more. He said he couldn't break his vows, no matter what was at stake."

Daisy added. "I think he must have heard something in a confession. Priests are very strict about not revealing anything they heard in confession."

"You think this is for real?"

"I don't know," said Fred. There was a pleading look on his face. The weight of what he'd told her was clearly bearing down him.

Isabel thought for a moment. "Did he say what was in those other letters?"

Fred shook his head. "No, all he said was that they're in Nuremberg, hidden in a place that is still the same since when I was there."

"Do you know where he meant?"

"No. I tried to figure it out, but I can't. Maybe I'm too old. There are a lot of places in Nuremberg untouched since the war."

"We thought you might help, because of your grandfather," said Daisy.

"How does this relate to my grandfather?"

Daisy stared at her husband. "Tell her, Fred."

"Your grandfather saw evidence of evil, which was never prosecuted," said Fred. "That's why he died."

"You know this for sure?" Isabel felt cold. This was the reason she had come here with them, why she hadn't left quickly, when they'd started spouting conspiracy theories about the Vatican. They were the first human connection she'd ever come across with the events that had shaped her family and who she was.

Her father had turned into an alcoholic. She always thought, at the back of her mind, that he'd been weakened, because his father had committed suicide. But she'd never understood why that dark event had happened. The thought that such things ran in families made her nervous sometimes too. Not often, just when her moods were bleakest.

She spoke slowly. Each word had weights attached to it. "You said the Nuremberg trials were fixed earlier, but you didn't say how. Tell me what you meant."

She had to understand.

Fred bit his lip. His eye lids were drooping. He looked fully his age, and sad. It took him another thirty seconds before he answered. "The trials were fixed, because some of the guilty men were never prosecuted," he spluttered, holding his chest.

"Why would this concern my grandfather so much?" Isabel said the words quickly. The truth was near and she had to grab at it before it disappeared.

"Because the person he was guarding, and questioning, was released without charge. It upset him greatly. He told me so. He even threatened to go public with what he knew." Fred and Daisy stared at her.

Why were they looking at her like that? She looked from one face to the other.

"You think my grandfather was murdered?"

Fred shrugged. Daisy just stared at her. Her hands were trembling in her lap.

"Who was he guarding?"

"I'll tell you, because you deserve to know, but you must understand, we have no evidence that your grandfather was murdered."

"Who was he guarding?"

"Cardinal Innitzer," said Fred. He spat the words out.

"He was Hitler's Cardinal," said Daisy, helpfully. "He signed a declaration endorsing Hitler's takeover of Austria in thirty-eight, five years after the first concentration camps were opened in Germany. Innitzer knew that Hitler was a mass murderer, but he still recommended him to the Austrian people. His letter was publicised all over Germany by Hitler too. It was proof that he had the support of the Catholic church."

Isabel's body tensed. "You think this Cardinal had something to do with my grandfather's death?"

They looked at each other. Fred answered. "We've long thought it."

She thought about everything they'd said. "Have you any idea what that priest meant by a new holocaust?"

Fred shook his head.

"This is a lot to take in," said Isabel. Memories of her father, drunk, when she was younger filled her mind.

"You tell me someone murdered my grandfather. Then you tell me there's another holocaust coming. And all you have to prove this, is a few pictures." She let out a soft, exasperated noise. Could all this be true? She could certainly feel their sincerity. What they'd said about her grandfather sounded right, but that didn't mean they were right about everything. What she needed was proof.

"Can you guess what's in the other letters," she said.

A gust of wind buffeted the window on Isabel's left. Daisy leaned forward. Isabel could smell moth balls. It was a faint smell, but it took her back to the house her grandmother had lived in, near Hampstead Heath. The place had a desolate feel to it every time she went there. It had been stuck in time, fading slowly.

"There's a lot of things people want hidden from the world. Millions of families were destroyed in the war. This letter shows us a glimpse of what really went on."

"Please, you have to do something," said Daisy. She looked tired, worn out by care.

"God only knows what the other letters might contain," added Fred. "And I hate to imagine what he meant by a new holocaust."

Isabel looked away from them, towards the view outside the window. It was dark now. The street lights were on and their glow smeared the glass, even from high up. It was time to go.

She released her hand from the arm of the chair, took her phone out of her bag.

"Do you mind if I take a snap of these?" She pointed at the yellowing pictures.

Fred nodded.

As she took close up pictures with her phone Daisy was coughing. Isabel offered to get some water. Daisy declined.

Isabel stood. One thought kept circling. Were they right about her grandfather?

It made her queasy to think that what had shaped her and her father, might have been a murder. She looked at her watch.

"You don't have anything else to show me?"

"No." Fred looked at his feet. Daisy started coughing again. This time she didn't stop.

Isabel knew she was outstaying her welcome, tiring them out.

"If you discover anything else, please email me or call me. This email address is secure. Only I can see what you send."

She passed her business card to Fred. He was standing near his wife now, leaning down towards her, his arm around her shoulder.

Daisy had a handkerchief to her mouth. The last thing Isabel saw, as she walked past her, was a red stain on the white cloth. A sickening sensation came over her. She'd seen this before. Her aunt had coughed blood the last time she'd visited her, before she'd died.

"Thank you for coming up. We'll be in touch again," were Fred's last words, before Isabel closed the door of the room.

She headed down to the reception. She'd texted David Wilkinson, a colleague from InfoFreed, when she'd been in the taxi coming to the hotel. She'd asked him to meet her in the main bar, near the reception, at eight.

She looked at her watch. It was ten past. Hopefully David had arrived. She would have to go home soon. But she had a duty to inform InfoFreed about what she'd learned in the meeting. Her job, initially for InfoFreed, had simply been to recover data on some hard drives that had been sent to them. A month later they'd asked her to be their IT manager.

Now she was involved in everything they did. Because there was only a few of them, that included meeting whistle blowers with secrets to share. InfoFreed had a protocol for every time such a contact was made. Simply put, a colleague had to be briefed, before and after, and a written online report logged.

She also had to work out if she should tell Sean what had happened. His decision to go to Nuremberg hadn't bothered her. She'd wanted to go with him, at first, because of the links the city had with her grandfather, but they'd decided it would be too much to bring Alek with them, and unfair to leave him alone unless there was a very good reason.

But something had begun to bother her about the trip as it approached, like a premonition. She ignored it, assuming it was just the fact that he was meeting an old girlfriend. But now she wasn't so sure. Maybe her premonition was something to do with the dark shadows from her family history, which were still unresolved.

She reached the hotel reception area a few minutes later. There were tourists and businessmen, and people dressed up, who looked like they were heading out for the night, and others, more dishevelled, arriving at the hotel to check in. The bar was busy too. Then she spotted David. He was waving frantically at her.

14

Sean put his hands up. The older officer clamped on steel handcuffs. They clicked tight.

"I haven't done anything," he said, his voice raised. "Who the hell has been murdered?"

"You know a lady called Eleni Kibre?" said the white haired policeman.

"Dear God, Eleni." He felt a dizzy sensation. He shook his head, took a step back. It felt as if the ground was falling, a part of the world disappearing under his feet.

The policeman was standing beside him. He pushed his chest out. It looked as if he was about to make a formal announcement.

"We need you to come to the police station to answer questions on this matter, Herr Ryan. I work for the USK, what you call a special police unit. We are investigating the murder of Professor Eleni Kibre, whose body was found in a car park behind her home two hours ago. From our information, Herr Ryan, you were the last person to see her alive."

There was a tightness in his throat, a dizziness spreading, but he stayed upright. The words he'd just heard seemed unreal, from a dream. It was impossible that Eleni was dead. Could they be mistaken?

"We will require your permission to take a DNA sample. Do you agree voluntarily to give us this permission?"

He looked at the police officer. The man's expression was hard, determined. Did he have to go along with everything these officers wanted? It felt as if they were rushing him. "And if I don't?"

"We have questions for you." The officer leaned close to him, until Sean could smell tobacco from the man's breath. "Why would you not agree, Herr Ryan? Do you have something to hide? It will better for you if you tell us everything."

Sean shook his head. "I've nothing to hide." A prolonged interview in a German police station was not what he needed right now.

"I'll give you the DNA sample," he said. The officer was right. It would look as if he was hiding something if he refused.

The Bundespolizei building Sean was driven to, with a siren blaring, was only five minutes away, still inside Nuremberg's walled old town. The building, a modern concrete office block, had a curved outer wall. A small Bundespolizei logo, a black eagle on a yellow background on the wall near a glass door, identified the building for what it was. They slowed as they approached.

Sean had enough experience of dealing with the police in various countries to know that being questioned was not the end of the world. But this felt different. The shock of hearing that Eleni had been murdered had not worn off. Memories of her were flooding through him, followed quickly by intense anger, and then a sense that this was all too unbelievable, filled him.

They couldn't be wrong about the identification, could they? A weight, a stone of guilt, formed inside him.

He should have advised her to take immediate action after she'd told him she was being targeted by extremists. He could have stayed with her longer, talked about what they could do. He should have taken it all more seriously. He should have gone to the police with them.

Could there be any other reason why she'd died?

The green-and-white police car went through a set of manned gates and into a small courtyard at the side of the building. Two of the officers walked Sean through a door with a security camera above it.

The black German imperial eagle on a yellow shield was repeated inside the building, on doors, walls, and in the elevator. The floors were highly polished, sparkling in places. As he followed the older officer he heard a muffled shout, from somewhere, then a door bang. The older officer, who'd identified himself as Inspekteur Bauer, stayed just ahead of him the whole time, turning and watching him occasionally.

Inspekteur Bauer informed him that he would be allowed to wait for consular support or a legal representative, if he wished, to have them present while he was being questioned. He declined.

"But I will ask for legal advice if this takes more than a few hours," he said. "I'm here to cooperate. I know nothing about her murder."

The room Sean was taken to, on the third floor, had no windows, four metal chairs screwed to the floor and a table fixed to the wall. It was unpleasantly stuffy. The smell of antiseptic hit his nostrils as soon as he entered it. He was left alone. To stew, he assumed. The black plastic dome of an observation camera made it clear he was being watched the whole time.

When Inspekteur Bauer returned, about twenty minutes later, he had a female police officer with him. She took notes during the interview and also started and later stopped, an audio recording device she placed on the table. She was broad shouldered, and had a purple birthmark the size of an orange on her neck.

The Inspekteur started the interview by asking Sean about the type of relationship he had with Eleni. There was something almost voyeuristic about his demands for information on exactly what had taken place between them fifteen years before, when they had both been in university in London.

"What's the purpose of all this questioning about my past?" said Sean. He looked at his watch. It was seven thirty. The awards ceremony and speeches were under way. He had managed to get permission from the Inspekteur, during the drive to the station, to text his contact at the conference, and he'd sent her a message that he wouldn't be able to make it *due to circumstances.*

It wasn't a good excuse, but he wasn't going to tell her he'd been brought in for questioning about a murder.

But Eleni had not only been murdered, she'd been violated. So he'd been told in the police car. That thought had made his stomach go cold.

When Sean kept asking about the purpose of the questions, where they were leading, Inspekteur Bauer left the room.

"I have to check something," he said. The female police officer followed him out without a word. Presumably to ensure nothing went on in the room while he was alone with just one officer.

It took fifteen minutes for them to come back. Sean had his elbows on the pale wooden table, and his head in his hands when they returned. He'd been wondering if Eleni's death had anything to do with him arriving in Nuremberg. He knew, rationally, that it couldn't be, but even contemplating it sent another wave of unease through him.

The Inspekteur hadn't answered his question about where Jerome was either. Sean assumed that they were still interviewing him.

He thought about Isabel, how she would react to the news. He'd asked for permission to text Isabel when he'd reached the station, but the request had been denied. He hadn't pressed for them to change their minds. He wasn't looking forward to telling her.

Now he couldn't contact her. His phone and wallet and some coins, all he had in pockets, had then been put in a see-through plastic bag, and he'd been given a receipt for them.

When the Inspekteur returned, he had pictures in his hand. Sean couldn't make out what was on them, but from the grim face of the Inspekteur he knew they wouldn't be pleasant.

"We have done some research on you, Herr Ryan. Your name is known to the authorities in England."

"Who told you this?"

"We receive cooperation on an Interpol level that might surprise you. When a murder is under investigation the cooperation is total." He sounded proud.

"What's my background got to do with Eleni?"

When Inspekteur Bauer handed the first photo to him, Sean thought he was going to throw up across the table. Acid rose in his throat, fast. Both the Inspekteur and the other officer watched him intently as he looked at the picture. He could sense them noting every twitch in his facial muscles.

The photos showed Eleni in her car. The driver's seat had been wound back. There was a dark patch of red on her jumper, where her heart was. What shocked him, though, was the mutilation to her forehead. Someone had sliced into her skin, all the way to the bone of her skull, exposing white patches mixed with congealing red blood.

The slices had been done in the shape of an arrow. His head pounded at the temples. His hands shook as he held the picture.

"Shocking, yes?" said the Inspekteur.

Sean nodded. He didn't want to talk. His mouth was paper dry. Memories of Eleni smiling only hours before were flashing through his mind. He saw her running her hand through her hair, smiling.

"Do you know why anyone would do this?" said the Inspekteur. "I think maybe this is something you know about. Yes?" He leaned towards Sean.

A flash of anger rose inside him. He had to force himself not to react. He'd have loved not to help this insulting Inspekteur.

When he spoke the words came out slowly. "I saw an arrow symbol, like this, here in Nuremberg earlier today." He put the picture down.

"Where was that?"

"At the Nazi Congress hall. In the basement. Eleni took me there."

"The basement area under the Congress hall is forbidden to the public. How did you get access?" The Inspekteur looked shocked.

Sean spent the next ten minutes explaining exactly what had happened, how Eleni had taken him to the Congress Hall, and every detail about what they'd done there, including that she'd suggested that the Nazis had been helped into power by the Catholic church.

At that point the Inspekteur shook his head.

"This is nonsense. These matters were dealt with long ago here in Germany." His expression was impassive, as if he'd seen far too many disturbing sights to be affected by what had happened to Eleni, or by what Sean had told him.

"It's nonsense?"

"This symbol is more properly related to some African superstition, I expect." the Inspekteur pointed at the picture.

Laurence O'Bryan

The female police officer was staring at him, as if he was a laboratory specimen. His skin crawled under her gaze.

"It's a universal symbol, Inspekteur. It's used by lots of cultures."

"Are you aware of its use in Africa rituals, Herr Ryan?"

15

The two-inch thick wooden door made a scratching noise against the floor as it opened. Xena hadn't heard the black suited priest approaching in the corridor. But she kept her head down, stared at his patent black shoes and black trousers. His shoes had thick rubber soles.

The priest coughed. She glanced up, looked down again, as a respectful nun was supposed to do. Her white wimple was tight against her chin and covered the front of her hair, but she pulled it another half inch forward with two thin fingers while she waited for him to speak.

It was unlikely he'd have a problem with the nun from Italy, even if she was clearly African. Her Italian was perfect and her letter of introduction simply asked for her to be allowed do some research for her doctorate in their 20th century document archive. The Diocesan Museum of Bamberg, fifty minutes' drive north of Nuremberg, had few items of value, and those, such as the Imperial star cloak, were on display on the floor above, not stored in this underground archive room.

"We are closing in thirty minutes, Sister." He smiled, thinly. "Are you staying in the convent?"

She shook her head.

He stepped forward, bent down to look at the yellowing magazines she had stacked in front of her.

"Are you sure these magazines will help you, Sister? Das Katholische Korps had a very limited run. It was closed by the Vatican in nineteen forty-four. I don't expect anything in there is of interest to someone pursuing church history. If I remember right it mostly contains lists of masses, and who was officiating." He went around the table to stand beside her.

"Ja, that is right. See." He pointed at the open magazine in front of her. Its thin pages were covered in a tiny German typeface, broken into three columns per page. Each column had a line drawing of a saint at the top with ornate, almost black, line drawings of the Holy Cross, and a Crown of Thorns above them.

Footsteps could be heard in the wide, flag-stoned corridor outside. He glanced at the still open door, as if afraid of being caught alone with the tall, thin, young nun.

He stepped back. "Thirty minutes, Sister. Then we will close."

The footsteps stopped at the door. She moved her hand to her thigh.

"Father." Came a thin voice, calling from the corridor.

As soon as he was gone Xena placed the magazine she had been poring over back in the middle of the stack, which she returned to the yellow cardboard box. She stood, went to the shelves and reinserted the box, moving some of the others, so he wouldn't be able to see which issues she'd been looking at.

She closed the door softly as she left. The priest was standing at the end of the corridor by the exit. He was waiting for her.

16

The Inspekteur picked up another picture from the small pile he had placed face down on the table and turned it over. It was a picture of a black boy's torso, the limbs cut off above the knees and elbows, and the top of the head sliced away above the ears. The torso was lying among long shiny leaves, in a jungle clearing.

Sean's skin prickled. The acid in his throat wanted to come up again. He swallowed fast. Why was the Inspekteur showing him this?

The cuts in the picture were weeping blood and the brain was exposed, a coiled gray rope. Sean wanted to look away, but he couldn't stop staring.

On the boy's chest an arrow symbol had been roughly cut deep into the flesh, exposing white bone in places.

"We do an international check on all symbols we find at a murder scene these days, Herr Ryan. Our computer systems are getting better. This came back straight away. The symbol was used during the massacres in Rwanda in nineteen ninety-four. You are old enough to remember that time, I am sure, ja?"

The Inspekteur was a real charmer. He could have taught arrogance at University level.

"I remember it."

"Did you know Jerome Ruzibiza, Eleni Kibre's boyfriend was a junior member of the Akazu, the Hutu extremist group who led the genocide against the Tutsi, and that his father was one of its leaders?"

That was the moment Sean felt the weight of suspicion shift, as if a cloak had been taken from his shoulders. He shook his head.

"Did Eleni speak to you about Jerome's background at all, Herr Ryan??

"No."

"Did either of them talk to you about African rituals or the occult?"

"We spoke about the occult when we were in the Congress hall. Eleni recited an exorcism prayer."

The Inspekteur paused. He looked satisfied with himself.

"Would you say she was obsessed by the occult?"

"I don't know where you're going with all this Inspekteur." Sean stared at him. "You're clutching at straws."

The Inspekteur's eyeballs had a metallic sheen.

"Did you hear Eleni and Jerome argue, Herr Ryan?"

Sean hesitated. The policewoman was staring at him. Her black plastic biro was poised above a page in her notebook. So, this was the real reason they'd shown him the photographs. They wanted him to incriminate Jerome.

"It wasn't an argument. It was more of a discussion. They were worried about neo-Nazi stickers on a street light outside their apartment. I already told you about them." Sean paused, looked down. Memories of what happened during his visit to Eleni's apartment came flooding back.

"Are you questioning the idiots who created those stickers? Jerome thought someone was targeting him and Eleni. Have you questioned the local neo-Nazi groups for suspects? I'd say that would be a good place to start your investigation."

"We have no neo-Nazi groups in Nuremberg, Herr Ryan. Your British media exaggerates such things. We have left-wing groups and right-wing groups and every shade in between. But none of them are neo-Nazi groups. You are mistaken. Such groups are banned in Germany."

Sean made an exasperated noise.

"Mistaken? I suppose that demonstration I saw earlier today in the centre of Nuremberg came from my imagination."

"No, this is not what I said. The march this afternoon here in this city was organised by the National Peace Party. We cannot say that the National Peace Party are a neo-Nazi party. I advise you not to listen to those who try to stir things up."

"But they marched to commemorate the bombing of Nuremberg." Sean's mouth opened. Could this guy be for real? The dress of the protestors, the confrontation between black-clad thugs and ordinary people, and the presence of anti-Nazi protestors, were clear evidence to him that the march had been what Eleni had told him it was: a march by neo-Nazis.

He leaned forward. How could they be in such denial?

"Do you still need me here, Inspekteur, if you think Jerome killed Eleni?"

"We do not confirm our suspects, Herr Ryan. And now." The Inspekteur leaned forward in his chair. He was half way over the table. His lips were pressed together, his head like a snake's moving in to strike. "When you saw Eleni Kibre and her boyfriend arguing, did you see any violence between them?"

"No. I didn't see any violence."

As Sean said it a flashback came to him. It was of Jerome swinging his arm, pushing Eleni, and Eleni backing away. He closed his mouth, stared hard at the Inspekteur, and felt the blood draining from his face. Could he be wrong about Jerome?

"Ah, you have remembered something, Herr Ryan. You must tell us. We take withholding information from the Bundespolizei very seriously in Germany. The offence is punishable by up to seven years in prison. You do not want to see our prisons, Herr Ryan. You will have a hard time with your talk of neo-Nazis there."

Sean looked straight ahead. He didn't want to hide anything, but the Inspekteur's keenness to find evidence against Jerome didn't feel right. Whatever he'd seen, it wasn't evidence of Jerome's violent inclinations. The tension in the room rose, as the Inspekteur stared at him.

Did he have an obligation to tell what he'd seen?

"Come, come, Herr Ryan. I see you have something you want to say." There was a hint of glee behind the steel in the Inspekteur's gaze.

The policewoman was writing furiously in her notebook.

"Where is Jerome right now?" said Sean.

"I can't answer this question. It is not permitted." The Inspekteur's tone was final, sharp, like a filing cabinet door slamming shut.

"If you decide to withhold information, I will arrange for a state lawyer to see you and for a place for you in the cells here, until the allocated lawyer arrives. I must warn you though, on a Saturday night it can take up to eight hours for one to come. Then we will have to arrange an official interview and an interpreter. Is that how you wish to proceed, Herr Ryan?" He looked at his watch.

Sean stared at him.

"I cannot stay here all night, Herr Ryan. I need to know what you are withholding from me."

Sean pressed his hands together, then rubbed them, as if to warm them.

"It was nothing. Jerome told Eleni to be careful, and he touched her arm, lightly, that's all. He was worried for her. I just thought he must have had a premonition, that's all I was thinking about. Go ahead, arrest me if you want to. I'll have nothing different to tell you tomorrow or whenever you interview me."

The Inspekteur looked at Sean, as if he'd told him a dead dog was under the table.

"I must press you again, Herr Ryan. Would you consider what Jerome Ruzibiza did intimidation, or physical violence, towards Eleni Kibre (as spelled above)?"

"No, Inspekteur. Definitely not. And I will give evidence to that effect, if needed," he replied, quickly.

They were in a staring match now. The other officer coughed. The Inspekteur turned to her and gave her a dismissive look.

"Inspekteur, may I leave now?" said Sean.

The Inspekteur turned back to face him. Then he looked at the pictures on the table and turned over the last one. For a moment Sean couldn't work out what was in the picture. It looked like a black club, something from a movie special effects department, with a vaguely familiar rectangle at the end.

Then he saw the stubs of fingers. It was an arm with the fingers cut off. It was sitting on a white plastic board. His pulse quickened. A squirming motion filled his stomach.

"Have you ever seen injuries like this, Herr Ryan?"

Sean couldn't answer. He suspected whose arm he was looking at, and where the tiny outcroppings of bone had been attached to only hours before.

"What is this?" He wanted to ask was this Eleni's arm, but the words wouldn't come out.

The Inspekteur was examining him. The policewoman was too. They both had an intense curiosity in their eyes.

"We do not know, yet," said the Inspekteur.

Sean shook his head. "This is sick." He paused. "Why would you would show me this, while my friend's body is still warm? I'm considering making a formal complaint, Inspekteur. Please take these pictures away." Those last words were spoken fast and loud. He didn't care what they thought. This was wrong.

The Inspekteur and the policewoman were still staring at him. "Please, answer our question, Herr Ryan. Do not assume you know whose arm this is." He turned the picture over, peered at a corner of it, then drew away. There was something printed there.

Sean moved towards the picture to get a clearer view. The Inspekteur let him get close, within about twelve inches, then he took hold of the picture and pulled it away from Sean's gaze. He handed it to the policewoman. He said something fast in German to her. She put the pictures under her arm, then exited the room.

"Our interview with you is finished, Herr Ryan." The Inspekteur said something official-sounding in German, then pressed a red button on the recording device.

While they walked to the front door of the station the Inspekteur said nothing. His final words to Sean were spoken in a dead, unemotional manner.

"We will contact you at your home in London, if we need any further information. Now you are free to go. Thank you for cooperating." He put his hand out and stiffly shook Sean's. As he did he clicked his heels together and bowed, just half an inch, but there was something formal and official about it.

Sean stepped out of the police station. Outside, there was an icy wind blowing. The street was deserted. He looked back at the station building. The glass door had already closed. Were they really letting him go so easily? As he looked up he saw a face at a window on the second floor. It was the face of the young officer. He was staring at Sean.

17

"Where the hell were you?" said David, as Isabel came towards him. He was sitting at a small table near the door to the bar in the Intercontinental Hyde Park Hotel, the remains of a pint of lager in front of him.

"Upstairs. What's the problem?" Isabel gave him her warmest smile. There was no reason for him to be so angry.

"I was worried."

"Why?"

"You've gone to meet an informant. Then you're late meeting me." He looked like a wounded dog.

"Let me get you another drink," she said. "I need one." She waved at a waiter, ordered a glass of Pinot Noir. The bar had a faux-Victorian style, all dark wood, deer heads and low glass chandeliers. Most of the tables were busy.

She told him everything that had happened.

"You're going to write all this up?" he asked.

Isabel nodded.

"Do you believe that stuff about your grandfather, that he was murdered?"

"I don't know. Honestly, it could be true or it could be a total fantasy." She shivered. Had she just been conned?

"But I have to find out the truth. I can't let this go." Something deep inside her had been touched. She sat straighter, then continued.

"My grandfather's death affected my whole family, David." She bit her lip. She'd said enough. Talking about it all made her feel angrier with every word.

"What about this other stuff, the letters that will incriminate the Vatican, do you believe all that? Do you think there are more of them?"

"Encouraging Hitler to attack Russia is bad enough, isn't it?" said Isabel.

"Most of the world was anti-Semitic back then. Racism was everywhere. You do know that, don't you?" He was leaning forward, to ensure the people around them didn't hear what he was saying.

"My family was lucky to be let into England in thirty-nine. Many of our relatives died in Auschwitz."

"I'm sorry."

"The whole world was guilty. That's what my father used to say."

He smiled at her. She got the sudden and disturbing notion that he liked her. She looked away. Across the room a large bald man in a black suit turned to look at her. He did it deliberately, as if he wanted her to know he was watching her. She remembered what she'd heard about the bars in big hotels being full of hookers. She stared at him, frowned, in distaste. He looked away.

"This place is full of creeps."

David shrugged. "Do you think they're right about a new holocaust being on its way?"

She was about to say something about pogroms happening in cycles, but the noise of an ambulance siren, whooping louder and louder, filled the room. Then it stopped. It seemed to be just outside the door of the bar. A blue flashing light filled the doorway.

People were craning to look. Seconds later two ambulance crew in green uniforms went rushing past the door. They were carrying a shiny steel gurney.

David was speaking. She looked at him. She hadn't heard a word he'd said. He smiled, leaned towards her.

She stood. "Sorry, David. I need to see what's happening."

He looked up at her, as if she'd grown an extra head.

18

The reception desk at Sean's hotel was empty when he passed by it. It was twenty-past ten on Saturday night, one hour ahead of London time. There wasn't even a receptionist manning the front desk. The elevator could only be accessed by using the room card he'd been given. There was a shiny plastic notice propped on the reception desk, in English and German, with a number to call in emergencies. Whether it was the number for the hotel staff in a back room or at the other side of town wasn't said.

Sean hadn't texted or called anyone during the taxi ride back. He'd been going over and over in his mind everything that had happened since he'd met Eleni. His light-headedness hadn't gone away. Looking out at strangers walking from one bar to another, or on their way home, made the ache of sadness inside him stronger. He was seeing the city for the first time.

He thought about calling Isabel, but decided against it. The last thing she would want to hear about would be the death of someone they knew in Nuremberg. He would break it to her in person after he got back to London. When he reached his room the TV was on, as were all the lights. The

TV had been switched to a German station. It came to him that someone had been in the room until a few minutes before. Had the police stayed, searching his room? He looked around, found no other evidence that anyone else had been there. He turned the TV off. Then he went to bed. He listened for hours to noises in the street, people shouting, cars passing.

He woke at six that Sunday morning, still exhausted. Thoughts about Eleni, and how she'd died, and the pictures the police had shown him, kept going around and around in his head, as if they would never disappear. There was no nice way to think about what had happened to her.

Were the police right, could Jerome be responsible? And if he wasn't, who had killed her, and why had they done it in such a grotesque manner?

He took a shower, hoping that his mind would clear. Maybe a shower would help get the sickening pictures out of his head, even for a few minutes. He wondered if attending the conference would help take his mind away from the images. There were a few lectures that afternoon that he could go to, and he could make his apologies for his non-attendance the night before in person.

As he dressed, he knew any enthusiasm for meeting people and putting on a front would be impossible for him muster. He looked at the conference schedule; perhaps he would attend just one lecture. He stood at the window and gazed out onto the busy avenue. Should he return to London?

Down in the breakfast room the TV was turned to a news channel. He ate a croissant and drank coffee as he watched it, even though it was all in German. He wondered if Eleni's murder would be featured.

A video clip showing the front of a kebab shop was playing. Then there were pictures of a body being taken to an ambulance in a green body bag.

Ein weiterer Türke ermordet, was the caption beneath the images.

He leaned over to a young man with close cropped hair sitting alone nearby. The man was also staring at the screen.

"Excuse me, what's happened?" asked Sean, pointing at the TV.

"Another immigrant dead," answered the man flatly. His English was heavily accented.

"We are going back to the past, ja," said the man. "It's how you say, a living nightmare, ja?" He looked at Sean for signs of agreement. "There are many foreigners living in our country these days. That's what's stirring this up all over again." He stood, waved at Sean as he left.

Distracted, Sean half waved in reply. He was thinking about how soon he'd be out of Nuremberg. His flight left at 10:50 the following morning. He would be back in London by lunchtime. Not a moment too soon.

He headed out into the street to get some air. The city had a deserted, lonely feel. He'd intended to do some sightseeing, but he didn't feel like going anywhere. He couldn't force himself to forget what had happened to Eleni. Everything else seemed totally unimportant.

An icy wind blew while he walked. Was Jerome still at the police station? He looked in his wallet. Jerome's card was still there, but the order of the credit cards, and recent business cards and receipts he'd picked up, looked different than it had the day before. He looked through the cards again. Yes, someone must have taken each of them out and looked at them. Each credit card number had probably been recorded and every phone number from the business cards too.

Were the *bundespolizei* going to track every cent he spent in Germany and every call he made?

He took Jerome's card out and punched in the number listed. To his surprise Jerome answered within two rings. He almost dropped his phone. He'd expected there to be no answer, expected to have to leave a message, for Jerome to be still in custody.

"Sean, it is so good to hear your voice." Jerome's was faltering, as if he'd been crying.

"I'm so sorry about Eleni. It's shocking. I can't believe it."

"You know what happened?"

"Yes, the police questioned me last night."

"Sean, please come to the Holiday Inn on Engelhardgasse. Room 213."

Sean hesitated.

"Where's that?

"Near the city center."

"I'll be there as soon as I can."

He turned toward the direction of the hotel and ordered a taxi. He was at Jerome's hotel twenty minutes later. It was still only ten-thirty. The Holiday Inn was on a narrow, brick-paved street with parking on one side. The hotel building was a cream colored modern copy of an older building, perhaps a building that was there before the war. It was part of a five story terrace of houses with two levels of attic windows jutting out from a steeply sloping tiled roof.

There were three square tables outside the hotel under canvas umbrellas. There was no one sitting at them. He went inside, headed straight for the elevator and up to room 213. The hotel reception was busy and no one even noticed him. His chest felt tight as he stood at the door of Jerome's room. There was no sound in the corridor. His knock was louder than he'd intended when his knuckles rapped at the pale wood of the door.

It was thirty seconds before Jerome answered. He called Sean's name, then opened the door when Sean replied. His face was a mess. It looked as if he'd been beaten up. There were large purple patches not only under his eyes, but also across his forehead and on his cheeks.

"Come in." He motioned Sean in, then poked his head out into the corridor.

Sean gripped Jerome's shoulder. After Jerome closed the door they hugged.

Jerome pulled away. His head went down.

"Are you okay?"

Jerome held out his hand. His breathing was laboured. He gripped Sean's when he extended it, held it like a lifeline. Then he turned away, a half suppressed cry of pain coming from somewhere deep inside him.

"They killed her. I told her they were going to do something bad. I told her a hundred times. No, two hundred." Jerome rubbed his palms across his face. The pressure made his skin buckle. He let out a scream. Strange African words flowed. Angry words. They echoed, then stopped. His voice faltered.

A television turned on in another room. The volume went up. Loud music thumped through the walls.

Jerome had his hands over his eyes. Tears appeared through the gaps between his fingers. Sean felt awkward, overwhelmed.

"The police think I had something to do with Eleni's death." Jerome pulled his hands away from his face. They cut through the air in front of Sean as he waved them about.

His expression was contorted again, this time in total supplication. "You must tell them I would never harm a single hair anywhere on her beautiful body. I would never do anything to the woman I love like my own life." He hit his chest with clasped hands. "They don't believe me!" Another half suppressed sob came from his throat.

"Did the police mistreat you?"

"No, no, but you must tell them I didn't do it. I couldn't do it. Please, Sean."

"I already told them that. I told them I'm sure you didn't do it."

"They asked you about me? When?" Jerome had a curious look on his face.

"Late yesterday afternoon. I was in the station for hours. I didn't get back to my hotel until nearly midnight."

Jerome's face darkened. "I was let out at six this morning."

"They're finished with you?"

"I don't know. They told me I could go. A young policeman came to the cell. He woke me. He almost pushed me out."

"They didn't tell you if they'd found the bastard who did it?"

"No. All he said was that they would visit me later today." He paused. "I can't go back to the apartment, Sean. I can't look at Eleni's things. I don't want to see them. You must understand that." He was pleading again. "I don't want to see the police again. Not now."

"They'll know you're here."

Jerome's eyes darted to the door. "I gave a false name at reception. I paid in cash." He looked unhappy.

"Why on earth, Jerome?" This was about the worst thing Jerome could have done. It would look as if he'd gone into hiding.

"I have to get things ready for her funeral. Her sisters must come. Her family must prepare her, prepare her apartment. They will stay there, turn her pictures to the wall, cover the mirrors. I cannot do these things. We were not married. Unless all this is done right her spirit will not return home. It will not return to Africa. It will be trapped here in Germany." He thumped his fist into his forehead. "I have to arrange so many things!"

It was hard for Sean to watch the scientist he'd spoken to the day before disintegrating in front of him. Jerome's grief was alive in the room, a presence. He looked twisted, both inside and out. Sean placed his hand on Jerome's arm. "I'm sure you'll have time to do everything right. She was a wonderful woman."

"She died in agony, Sean! Her spirit cries for vengeance." Jerome's face was twisting again. This time he looked angry, almost out of control. He sat, abruptly, leaned back, put his hands out wide. The chair creaked.

"I do not know if her sisters will come. They are poor. I must decide too many things!" He raised his hands to the roof. "I should have saved her. I could have."

Sean sat in the other chair. "Please, Jerome. You're not responsible for what happened. Someone did this to her. The police will find them. I will help you, if you need money."

"Thank you, but no. I will be fine." He turned to Sean. "Do you think they will find who killed her?" He laughed manically. "Because I don't. They asked me if Eleni was involved in occult practices, devil worship, that kind of thing. I nearly hit them. Those policemen are evil. They asked, did she have African friends, groups that she used to meet. They want to blame us. I told them about the stickers. They say they are everywhere." He wrung his hands.

"They kept asking about her friends and her family, what their beliefs are." He banged his hands into his face, held them there. They were shaking. His bones were moving under his skin. His voice thickened.

"They wouldn't listen. I told them the evil of their Nazi grandfathers has come back, because of all the refugees that have come here. I told them I can feel the hatred in this country growing every day. They just sat there, staring at me." He grimaced. "Then they asked me again about what I knew about the occult." Spittle flecked the air. His hands were fists. His eyes were blazing.

"Eleni was supposed to do an interview with a journalist, about how Adolf Hitler was a front." He lifted his hands, as if controlling a marionette.

"A front for who?" It sounded implausible.

"The Vatican." He spat out the word. "That's where Hitler got his hatred of the Jews. You know Pope Paul IV began this thing of forcing Jews to wear yellow stars in 1555, and he forced the Jews to all be locked in ghettos at night, in every Christian city. The Vatican wanted the Jewish ghettos back for decades before Hitler followed their ideas. He said this himself!" He paused, reached a hand out towards Sean.

"Somebody must have found out what Eleni was going to broadcast! That's why they murdered her." His eyes were wide, bloodshot. His hands were shaking.

"Have you slept?" Sean was concerned for Jerome now. He pulled his chair closer. They were only a few feet apart.

"No, no, I can't sleep. What they did to Eleni makes me sick. It makes me want to die! The police told me everything. They wanted to know had I heard of such rituals!" He leaned forward, then back, rocking.

Sean leaned in towards him. "You should rest," he said, gently. "Would you like me to call a doctor, get you a sleeping pill?"

Jerome didn't seem to hear him.

"The genocide. It's starting again," he said. He raised his fists in front of him. "I can feel it."

"You can't say that, just because of Eleni."

"Yes, yes, I can. And I will. I didn't tell you everything yet." His fists dropped. He had a beaten look on his face.

"What didn't you tell me?"

Jerome glared at him. "There's a story going around among all of us Africans here in Nuremberg."

Sean shook his head. "You can't believe in rumors."

"But this one is coming true." Jerome raised a hand to him. "They're going to try to kill all Africans next."

"That's just paranoia."

"That's what the Jews said, before they were all rounded up." Jerome was angry. He raised a fist to his forehead, held it there, pressing into his skin, crinkling it.

There was silence in the room. Then Jerome let out a long sob, which became a moan.

"I'm so sorry," said Sean.

A warbling sound filled the air. It was Sean's phone. He slipped it from his pocket awkwardly, almost dropped it, put it to his ear.

"Sean?" It was Isabel's voice.

"Hi. Is everything okay?" he said.

"Something strange just happened," she said.

19

Xena was in the ground floor reception area of a two storey building in the Nordend suburb of Frankfurt. The building had no markings on it to say who occupied it. The security guard who'd opened the glass door to allow her inside was standing behind a low desk. He had his phone to his ear.

He'd stared at her Ethiopian bracelets as she'd moved past him, and had spent longer than he should have looking at her braided cornrow hairstyle, and admiring her tight jeans.

He'd advised her to sit and wait on one of the cream leather sofas that filled one corner, by the floor-to-ceiling glass windows. The windows had thick metal blinds blocking out the view. The only sound in the reception area was the faint hum of air conditioning. The only smell was lemony antiseptic, as if the last people who'd been here had been cleaners.

But Xena didn't sit. Nervous energy moved inside her. She went to the far wall, where there was a shiny red fire extinguisher, then paced around the sofas, then headed back to the fire extinguisher.

From a distance, the way she was dressed, you might have assumed she was meeting a lover or a husband, that she was rich and admired, a model perhaps, or a diplomat's daughter. Her eyes gave no hint of what she did best.

"Fräulein," said the security guard, as he walked towards her.

"Yes," said Xena. Her German was as good as her Italian and her English, but she preferred for some people to think she couldn't understand them. She also spoke Amharic and Oromo, the two main languages of Ethiopia.

"Please go to the second floor," he said, in English. He pointed at the elevator.

As the elevator went up Xena recited her prayer.

"Abba-Ta-Chin, Hoy Besemay Yemit'Nor," it began. *Our Father, who art in Heaven.*

Her words grew softer, barely audible.

When the elevator doors opened with a sigh, she stepped forward. There was an ebony-black reception desk at the far side of a white carpeted area. No one was waiting there. She looked around, saw a half-open door to her left and headed towards it.

A tall man, with a nut-brown, wrinkled face stood beyond the doorway. His expression was gloomy. His neck muscles bulged over the white collar of his shirt and his suit jacket fitted him too tightly. Xena knew this was a dress statement by security guards here in Germany, many of them ex special-forces, since the refugee riots across Europe had begun. They liked to show off their physiques.

"Please, I must search you." His English was good, but his German inflections were hard to hide.

Xena shrugged, kept her expression firm, put her arms out to her side.

The guard gave her a pat down. He missed the paper-thin knife inside her thigh, near the top. He checked her small leather shoulder bag, verified that the phone inside worked. She'd expected he wouldn't find the knife. He'd have had to strip search to do that. Its shape was curved at the edges and its handle was as thin as the blade.

When he was finished, he nodded, and let her pass.

Vanessa Sheer was at the far end of the room, standing beside a wall of windows overlooking the Main River. Below, the water was a dark band, a hundred metres wide. Beyond it were the lights of the skyscrapers of Frankfurt's financial district. They twinkled like columns of jewels. A laser beam from one of the buildings lit the low clouds overhead with blue circles.

"Welcome back to Frankfurt, Fräulein," said Sheer. She walked fast towards Xena, her hand out straight in front of her.

It felt cold when Xena grasped it. But she shook it firmly, and squeezed it. Vanessa pulled her hand away.

"Come, sit. Tell me what progress you have made." Sheer pointed at a gray leather sofa in the far corner of the room. Two leather chairs faced it, making a meeting area. The only other furniture in the room was a black wooden desk with a thin silver screen on it.

Xena sat, her long legs spread wide in front of her. "The job is done. The name Catherine was mentioned. I believe he meant St. Catherine's."

"Good work," said Vanessa. "But we have another problem."

Xena stared back at her. "What problem?"

"Sean Ryan." Vanessa's eyes flicked to the door at the far end of the room. A tall figure with silver gray hair, Monsignor Salerna, was standing in the doorway, observing them.

Vanessa stood, motioned the priest forward.

"I will need another payment."

There was a languid tone to Vanessa Sheer's voice when she responded. "You will get it, when the problem has been solved."

Xena put her hand out. "And today's payment?"

Vanessa went to the desk, opened a drawer, took out an envelope and passed it to Xena. Xena opened it, flicked through the notes inside. She peered closely at one of the notes, then nodded, closed the envelope, pocketed it.

"Call me on the secure line as soon as you confirm the problem is solved. Sean Ryan is in Nuremberg until tomorrow. His hotel is the Centrum, on Augustiner Strasse. Get it over with quickly." She didn't offer her hand as Xena moved to the door.

When she was outside the building Xena looked back. The security guard who'd been in the reception area was gone and the lights were out. The building looked deserted.

Perhaps it had only been opened for their meeting. She walked fast. She'd parked her hire car three blocks away.

The drive to Nuremberg would take a little over four hours. She would watch for unmarked police cars, but she would be doing nothing that would attract their attention.

What she had to do on the journey was work out a good way to finish this job properly.

20

Sean held the phone tight to his ear. He could hear Isabel breathing. Jerome was staring at him. He glanced around. He needed some privacy. Jerome must have sensed it. He walked towards the bathroom. As the door closed behind him, Sean spoke.

"What happened? Is Alek okay?"

"No, it's not Alek."

"Is this about Eleni?"

There was a pause. He could sense Isabel's mind ticking over.

"What happened to Eleni?"

There could be no avoiding it now.

"She's been murdered." He heard a gasp, the sound of Isabel sucking in her breath. He closed his eyes. He felt guilty for worrying her.

"When are you coming home, Sean?" The worried note in her voice was like a hand squeezing Sean's heart.

"About seven tomorrow night."

"How did Eleni die?" There was almost an accusation in her question.

"She was being harassed here. It looks like some neo-Nazis did it. The whole thing is horrific. I'm with her partner right now."

"Make sure you come home tomorrow, Sean. Please. There's something we need to talk about."

He heard the shower starting in the bathroom. He went to the window overlooking the street. Cars were moving slowly.

"What is it we need to talk about? Is everything okay?"

"I'll tell you when I see you. I just wanted to check you were okay."

"I am." He heard her breathing.

"Is Eleni's partner okay?"

"No, he's not. I should go, Isabel." He was tempted to press her about whatever was going on back in London, but he'd heard a thud from the bathroom.

He ended the call, knocked on the bathroom door. There was no answer. All he could hear was the water from the shower hammering down. He knocked again. Still no answer. He stood there. Anxiety for Jerome rose inside him.

He called out, louder this time. The water stopped. Jerome replied.

"Please, wait downstairs, Sean. I'll be down in twenty minutes. I want to take you somewhere that will blow your mind."

Sean stood at the door, wondered if he should stay in the room.

"Sean, are you there?" Jerome sounded worried.

He put his hand on the door.

"I'll be downstairs," he said.

"Thanks, Sean. You're a true friend. Eleni was right." There was an emotional rawness in Jerome's voice.

He waited, pacing, in the lobby. It had leather chairs, a rack of tourist literature, pictures on the walls, sights of Nuremberg from before the war. The receptionist, a thin man who could have been Spanish or Italian, barely looked at him. Sean could see the street outside. He stood by the window. Yes, he was right, that was Eleni's car on the other side.

The green BMW stood out among the newer cars. Was Jerome driving it? Where was he intending to take him? Sean sat down. What else could he do to help Jerome?

The first thing he'd have to do would be to find out exactly where Jerome was taking him, and why. If the police were looking for him, the best thing would be for Jerome to call them, tell them where he was staying, what he was up to. He had to avoid any more suspicion falling on him.

Minutes passed. A fluttering sensation started in his stomach. It got worse when a police car appeared outside, moving slowly down the street, stopping occasionally, as if they were looking for something. Then the car stopped in front of Jerome's, blocking it in. Sean couldn't see inside, but he could imagine the officers reporting that they'd found a car they'd been looking for. It stayed for only a minute though. Then it rolled on.

He was definitely going to get Jerome to call the police before he went anywhere with him. He looked at his watch. It was five past twelve. He'd been waiting well over twenty minutes. He looked at his watch again. Two men, both wearing blue boiler suits, had come into the foyer. One of them leaned over the reception desk, showed something to the receptionist. The man nodded, pointed at the elevator. Sean took out his phone, checked his email messages.

He sent two replies to colleagues at the institute. Both of them wanted to know how his speech had gone at the conference. Both of them also made passing reference to the meeting on Tuesday. He sent replies to each, telling them the same story, that Eleni had died and he wasn't able to give his speech. He also told them he hadn't decided whether he was going to come to the Tuesday meeting.

He smiled as he sent the emails. Both of the people he'd responded to were friends of the director of the institute. They were both clearly fishing for information. It would be good if they thought he wouldn't make the meeting. He could surprise them.

He looked up, glanced out the window. The BMW was gone. At first it didn't register in his mind what that might mean, then he glanced back at the empty space across the road. Had Jerome gone past him? No, that was impossible. He'd looked up each time the elevator had opened. That had only been two or three times in the past few minutes.

He took his mobile out, called Jerome's number.

There was no answer.

He stood, went to the reception desk, asked for Jerome's room to be called. The man obliged. They both waited as he held the phone to his ear.

Eventually he put it down. "I am sorry, there is no answer. The guest must be out." The man looked over Sean's shoulder. Sean turned. There was a family group waiting patiently behind him. It looked as if they were checking in.

He stepped aside.

Sean spent the next few minutes looking at his watch, debating with himself whether to keep waiting or go back up to Jerome's room. He called Jerome's mobile two times while he waited. There was no answer. He couldn't wait any longer. He went up in the elevator.

The wait outside Jerome's door seemed interminable. He'd knocked loudly three times. Then he knocked again. There was still no answer. He tried the door handle. His hand felt clammy. He heard a voice behind him. He turned, fast. There was a cleaning lady in the corridor. She'd appeared from a room two doors down.

She repeated what she'd said, but as it was in German, he had no idea how to respond. The woman smiled.

"Lost key, ja?" she said.

He shrugged. "Sorry, no. I'm looking for this man." He pointed with his thumb at the door of Jerome's room.

The woman looked at him oddly. "Man here go out," she said. "With his friends."

"When?" said Sean, surprised. He took a step back. Jerome had gone off with someone? Why hadn't he told him?

The woman shrugged. She didn't understand his question. Had he missed them when he came up?

A few minutes later he was at the reception desk again asking if anyone had seen Jerome or left a message for a Sean Ryan. The man who'd been there was gone. Instead there was a thin blond woman. Her English was poor. Sean told her Jerome's name, wrote down the room number. She rang Jerome's room, then shrugged and said, "Er muss gegangen," twice, for added effect.

Sean just looked at her.

"Er muss gegangen," she said for a third time.

"I'm sorry, I don't speak German," he said.

A voice called out behind him.

"She says the person must have gone out."

Sean turned. A small man, he looked like an academic, was standing nearby. He smiled at Sean. "You were looking for someone, yes."

"Can you ask her is there a message for me? My name is Sean Ryan."

"Ah, Herr Ryan. We missed your speech last night. It was much anticipated." The man held his hand out to Sean.

Sean shook it. "I'm sorry I couldn't make it. Someone I know has died."

The man stepped around Sean, spoke fast in German to the receptionist. She looked down at her desk, shook her head.

The phone she'd been using warbled insistently. She picked it up.

"Ja."

Sean watched as her skin tone changed from honey brown to pale in a few seconds, and her jaw drop, almost comically.

The phone almost slipped from her fingers. She replied briefly in German, in a high pitched tone, then slammed the phone down. She picked it up again immediately and stabbed her fingers at the buttons.

Sean and his new friend watched her. When she spoke it was in a rapid-fire stream of German with the phone in her cupped hand.

The man behind Sean let out a loud sigh. "It seems a cleaner has found blood and some damage in one of the rooms. Perhaps you can come back later, Herr Ryan." He raised his eyebrows. That was when he saw the woman's finger come up and point at him. It seemed as if she was talking about him on the phone.

"The police are coming," said the man. He was staring at Sean now as well.

Sean turned to him. "Thanks." He headed for the door.

The police would know soon enough that he'd been here, but he didn't care. He didn't want to wait for them either. He had to get out of there. He needed to think. He walked up the street. What the hell was going on? He looked over his shoulder, half expecting to see Jerome appear. Wishful thinking, he knew, but he couldn't help it. When he reached the next corner he saw the police car he'd seen earlier, or one just like it, coming towards him.

Its blue roof light came on. The light bounced off the shop windows as it passed him, startling him. Then its siren turned on. A sickening dread grew into a knotted ball inside his stomach. The siren echoed through the street. He stopped, half expecting the police car to stop too, for a policeman to jump out and run towards him. Blood was pounding through his forehead. But they didn't stop. They headed past him towards the hotel.

Sean turned left, kept walking. He didn't know where he was going. He would have to go to the police, he knew that, but he needed time to clear his head.

What the hell had happened to Jerome?

21

Vanessa Sheer pressed the switch, which turned on the voice encryption system. Then she dialled the number. Below, in the street, a green BMW passed by, slowly.

"Doctor Fleischer, have you checked your security systems?"

The encryption device ensured that not one of the possible dozen security services agencies interested in her would understand what they were talking about. All an eavesdropper would hear would be a recording of a bland conversation played over the ordinary telephone line. The digitally encrypted call would be static in the background.

"I have."

"Good. There can be no mistakes." She sat on the shiny steel and leather chair and put her right elbow on the ebony hotel suite desk. She held the phone tight to her ear.

"You have started the disbursement, ja?"

"Ja, we have tested this in each location. The refugee children will consume the bread, and the parents will bring what is left back to their homes to be eaten later."

"The delivery method is secure?"

"Ja, the items were hand delivered by our courier. The gift was made before with no ill effect, so nothing will be suspected this time."

"I am counting on you not to have made any mistakes, Herr Doctor." She didn't sound nervous. It sounded as if she was reminding him of his duty.

"No test has yet been devised to identify what we have infected the bread with."

"I hope the dispersal pattern will be as you predicted."

"I expect some of the carriers will be quarantined, but enough will not. I can assure you we have targeted a sufficient percentage of the group."

"This is a good day, Herr Doctor. Your role in this will be remembered. We are the only ones who are strong enough, determined enough, to clean up the mess our weak and stupid politicians have left us with."

"Thank you, Frau Sheer."

"Your work on the other variants of the pathogen is complete?"

"Ja."

"Good. The dregs of this world must be washed away as quickly as possible, everywhere." She paused, glanced at her silver laptop sitting open on the table. "It will be interesting to see how quickly the news media gets to hear of this."

The doctor grunted. "Terrorists will be blamed. One group of refugees fighting another. It is the easy answer for lazy journalists."

She didn't tell him that one of the board members of BXH in Germany controlled one of the largest media empires in

Europe. His stations and online outlets would be blaming external forces outside Germany, for stirring up murderous rivalries between refugee groups.

"All the deliveries have been done?"

"All will be finished within the next thirty minutes."

"Sehr gut."

22

Sean walked for half an hour. The city had woken up. Restaurants and a few shops were open now. He didn't stop at any of them. If Jerome had also disappeared that could mean he was going to be murdered, just as Eleni had been. There was an acid taste in his mouth. He felt dizzy at the thought of what might be happening to Jerome at that moment.

He remembered the two men who had gone up in the elevator. Had they come after the police car? He wasn't sure. But one thing was sure, he would have to go to the police station soon. He'd probably be arrested at the airport if he didn't.

He put a hand in his pocket. The Inspekteur who had interviewed him had given him a card. He found it. He called the number.

A man's voice answered. It wasn't the Inspekteur's.

"Do you speak English?" he asked.

"Yes."

"This is Sean Ryan," he said. "I have some information about the disappearance of Jerome Ruzibiza."

Laurence O'Bryan

There was a pause. He heard clicking, the sound of someone tapping at a keyboard.

"Herr Ryan," said the voice. "Where are you?"

"I don't know." He looked at the wall at the corner of the street. There was no street name there. "I will come to the police station. I'll be there soon."

"Good. We will be waiting for you." The line went dead.

Waiting with lots of questions. He saw a taxi, waved at it. The driver didn't see him. He turned into a bigger road ahead on the right. Maybe the taxi driver had seen him and just didn't want to stop. Had the police put out an alert for him?

He took his phone out of his pocket, pressed the button on the top. They might be able to track him from the call he'd made, but at least with it off, they would have some difficulty finding out where he was going before he went to the station.

He turned onto another street lined with shops, saw another taxi cruising. This one stopped for him. He was back at his hotel five minutes later. He'd been nearer than he'd thought. He went to his room, packed his bag. If the police planned to interview him for longer this time he wanted to have everything ready to leave the hotel when he needed to.

He left his room key at reception and headed out.

He asked the next taxi driver to follow the tram tracks out of the city. He'd figured out which tram line Eleni had lived on. It became confusing when two tram lines diverged, but after heading down the wrong one for a few minutes he told the driver to go back until they found the other one, line four, and follow it again.

When they reached Eleni's apartment building he told the taxi driver to wait. The man had no English, but he nodded when Sean said, "Funf minuten, bitte."

He wanted to take pictures of the stickers outside Eleni's apartment. They would be something tangible to show the police how she was being harassed. He went straight to the lamp post he'd seen the sticker on.

It was clean. Not even the little bits of the stickers that they'd left behind the following day remained. He looked on the next lamp post, just in case, but there was nothing there either. He went to the door of their apartment building, found the right bell, pressed it. Then he waited.

No one came. He pressed it again. It had been a long shot that Jerome would be here.

He looked up at the windows opposite, saw a lace curtain flicker. He was being watched. He crossed the street, looked back at the building Eleni and Jerome lived in. He stared up at the apartment he'd been in only the day before. He wasn't sure what he was looking for, but he glanced up again at the building he was now beside, to see if he was being watched. But no lace curtain moved this time.

As he turned back he saw movement in the window of Eleni's apartment. Someone had passed the window. Was it Jerome?

He went to the door, pressed his finger to the buzzer, held it there. After thirty seconds he let it go. The taxi driver was staring at him from the far side of the street.

Then the door opened. A large man with long black hair said something fast and unfriendly to him in German. Then he moved to close the door in Sean's face. Sean put his foot against the door.

"Is Jerome here?" he said.

"What you want?" said the man. He was barring the door with his bulk, as if his life depended on it.

"Who are you?" said Sean.

"Caretaker. Jerome, he run away." He made a waving gesture with his hand, then sneered, as if Sean was a dog pissing on his doorstep.

Sean wanted to react, but arguing in broken English with this idiot wasn't going to achieve anything. He shook his head, turned away, headed back to the taxi. The driver had the engine running. He tried to read the address of the police station out to him, but in the end he just handed the Inspekteur's card over. The driver nodded, suddenly serious, and gave the card back to Sean. He looked at Sean warily after that.

After he dropped Sean at the door of the police station, Sean looked back. The taxi driver was hunched over. He appeared to be writing something.

"Don't get paranoid," he said, to himself

Thirty minutes later he was wondering if he'd been wrong about that. He was taken within seconds of his arrival to a different interview room to the one he'd been in before. This one had a metal table and four metal chairs, painted yellow. They were all screwed into the painted concrete floor.

"Why did you visit the apartment Eleni Kibre lived in thirty minutes ago?" said the young police officer who was interviewing him. His English was almost perfect.

"Your information is very up to date."

The officer didn't smile. He simply repeated the question.

"I went to see if the neo-Nazi stickers I'd seen yesterday were still there."

The policeman took his time responding. There was no other officer in the room with them this time. The security camera high in one corner was probably recording everything. It glared back at them.

"Why do these stickers interest you?"

"My friend has been murdered." He paused. "If that happened to a friend of yours, wouldn't you be interested in the intimidation she was being put through?"

"You know who murdered her?"

"It wasn't her partner. I know that."

"In sixty-five percent of murders in Germany, the victim knows the perpetrator. You have the same in your country, I think."

Still no smile.

"What makes you think her partner didn't do it?" He raised his eyebrows. He seemed to be hoping that Sean would reveal something.

"It seems too convenient."

"The obvious is sometimes the best answer, Herr Ryan. Didn't one of your famous detectives say that?"

"He was a fictional detective."

The officer gave Sean a look that said, I know that.

"His observation was correct though."

Sean coughed. The disinfectant smell in this interview room was even more powerful than in the other one the day before.

"Are you looking for Jerome Ruzibiza?"

"We do not discuss operational matters in these cases."

"But you have to be looking for him. He's gone missing."

"We cannot say what has happened to Jerome Ruzibiza, whether he is missing or not."

"He's not a murderer. And something has happened to him. I was at his hotel this morning."

The policeman's mouth twitched. His expression indicated he already knew where Sean had been that morning.

"Tell me what happened there."

Sean told him.

"Have you found Jerome?"

The officer shrugged. "I do not know that, Herr Ryan."

"Aren't you concerned about what may have happened to Jerome Ruzibiza?"

"A report was filed by the hotel about damage to his room. We are looking into it."

"That doesn't sound very urgent."

"We cannot know what has happened to Jerome Ruzibiza, Herr Ryan. We have very little to go on. He may have gone away with friends to visit his own people. We have to do these things correctly. There are procedures that have to be followed. I am sure you understand."

Sean looked at the officer.

"This is just time-wasting." The officer shrugged. "I don't know about your procedures, but Jerome Ruzibiza's life is in danger. I am sure of that. You can't just shrug this off."

The officer stood. "Jerome Ruzibiza has recently lost his job here in Germany, Herr Ryan. His partner has also died. I have experience with immigrants and refugees. Such things often lead to them returning to their country. Perhaps it is for the best." He smiled for the first time in their conversation.

Sean stared at him. "You're not taking this seriously at all," he said.

"You may leave now, Herr Ryan." He opened the interview room door.

Sean stood. "Are you investigating the Nazis who left stickers outside Eleni and Jerome's home?"

The officer shook his head. "We have no reports of intimidation from their apartment block. I think you are mistaken, Herr Ryan. Several rock groups use such symbols to create a little, what do you English call it, buzz. I am right, am I not?" He smiled, condescendingly.

"This was nothing like that." Sean was angry now. How could this guy be so pig-headed? "He and Eleni were in fear of their lives and look what's happened." His voice was raised.

The policeman's face hardened. "If you have any other information about Eleni Kibre's disappearance, Herr Ryan, please contact us." He opened the door of the interview room, stood holding it for Sean to pass.

As they went down the corridor a small man in plain clothes came out of a room and said something to the officer with Sean, which he replied to. It sounded like an irritable exchange.

In the brick walled reception area the officer clicked his heels. "Goodbye, Herr Ryan. If we need to contact you again we will do so."

And that was it. Sean felt at a loss when he went out into the street. He'd expected the police to be more interested in him and in the intimidation Eleni and Jerome had suffered. It seemed as if they'd already made their minds up about what had happened.

A man was standing behind the glass door of the station looking at him. It was the same man who'd been talking to the officer who'd interviewed him before. Sean kept walking. Who could you go to in Germany, if you didn't trust the police? But more importantly, what the hell had happened to Jerome?

Sean knew the way back to the hotel now, he'd taken the journey so often. He started walking. Cars streamed by him. What was left for him to do? He'd been to the apartment. He'd seen the police. Should he go back to Jerome's hotel, to check if he'd reappeared? He took out his phone, opened the web browser, put the name of the hotel in. Their web site came up. He called the number.

Jerome wasn't there. He wasn't even registered as a guest anymore.

It was three-thirty when he arrived back at his own hotel. He looked in the door of the restaurant, but he didn't stay. He had no appetite. He headed up to his room. He was about to open his laptop when a sharp knock sounded on his door.

He opened it, half expecting policemen in uniform to be standing there again. But they weren't. It was the man, a plain clothes officer, he presumed, who had been watching him at the police station.

"I think I've answered every question I can, officer," he said. He held the wooden door half closed.

"I know that, Herr Ryan. My name is Kurt Dienelt. I am here to help you."

"How?"

"To help you find your friend." He pronounced friend as if it had a u in the middle.

Kurt had thin blond hair, and bags under his eyes that gave him a weary look. He reminded Sean of movies with German intellectuals in them.

"May I come in, Herr Ryan?"

Sean opened the door to let him pass. He noticed a small brown holster on Kurt's belt.

"I hoped I would see you earlier, but I was delayed with other matters."

Kurt Dienelt sat at the small wooden breakfast table. Sean pulled the orange curtains open a bit more and sat down opposite him.

"Do you know something about Jerome's disappearance?"

Kurt leaned forward. "I do." The low hum of cars outside in the street filled the room.

In his mind Sean could see images of what had been dome to Eleni. He imagined the same thing happening to Jerome. Had the police shown Jerome the pictures too? For a few seconds he imagined himself in that situation. His muscles tightened and a shiver of darkness passed through him.

He wanted to shout at Kurt, to get him to tell what he knew and quickly. Instead he just stared at the officer.

"You must prepare yourself."

"Why?" Sean pressed his lips together. He sucked in air, tightened his fists as he did so.

Kurt sighed, shook his head.

23

The small home office room in Sean and Isabel's house felt gloomy. Most of the time it was filled with the empty hum of passing cars from the street below. Dirty gray clouds covered the Sunday afternoon London sky like a lid. Isabel was examining her hands. They were trembling. She gripped them together.

The laptop screen in front of her blinked as it reloaded a web page with a large image in its centre, showing the Nazi hierarchy in the dock, including Herman Göring, the most prominent Nazi to stand trial at Nuremberg. A row of white helmeted U.S. military policemen stood to attention behind him.

This was the iconic image of the trials, which lasted almost a year and ended with the individual sentences being read out on the afternoon of October 1, 1946. The image didn't show her grandfather, Philip Sharp, nor did it show Colonel Geoffrey Lawrence, the President of the Nuremberg Tribunal, the lead British Judge, who her grandfather had been guarding.

Her grandfather had been serving as a lieutenant with the Royal Artillery Military Police at that time. He'd landed in

France a week after D-Day, and had managed to make it all the way to Germany without suffering anything more than a few bruises, so his diary claimed. Then he was promoted to a Close Protection Unit.

He was dead before Christmas '46.

Isabel took a manila folder from the bottom of the book case and opened it. Inside was a black leather Letts diary, and a few letters on yellowing, almost see-through paper. The diary was breast pocket-sized and a half-inch thick. The cover had *1946* embossed on it in now-fragile gold leaf. She lifted the diary, felt the crinkled leather cover shift under her fingers. The spine was cracked through. Frayed brown cardboard poked out at the corners. The years between her and the war slid away as she held it, transporting her back to London in '46, a city on rations, rebuilding slowly after the destruction the Luftwaffe had inflicted on it.

She opened the diary at the entry for December the 12th, a Thursday. A faint dusty smell, with a hint of cordite, came to her as she raised the diary, to read the handwriting again. The entry, in dark blue ink, read:

...

If people knew the sickening depravities of the defendants, and of those others who should have been charged at Nuremberg, and the evil of their crimes, most reasonable people would not be able to sleep, as I am unable to.
What I saw and heard here in Nuremberg, and what I learned of the support the Nazi regime received in surprising places, has sickened my mind.

I apologise to my wife and children for any suffering I inflict.
I love you all dearly, far more than I can say.
> *Yours Regretfully,*
> *Philip Sharp,*
> *Lt. Royal Artillery.*

Faded, brown rimmed splotches, stained the page, as if tears had fallen on it a long time ago.

Her father had given her the diary just before he'd moved to India, saying: "Your grandfather was a real hero." They'd all assumed that the passage from his diary was a suicide note. It had cast a long shadow over their lives.

But was it a suicide note? They were certainly the words of someone under stress, but he could have been talking about other pains he might inflict, not suicide.

And what had her grandfather meant by *"the support the Nazis received"*? Was he talking about the Catholic Church?

She pushed her hair behind her ears, looked through the other entries in the diary. All the writing was small, and mostly in blue ink. One name stood out. It had been underlined three times. She turned to her laptop and looked it up.

The sentence read – *I wish I'd never met Orsenigo.*

She read the references in Google and followed the most likely one to an article about Cesare Orsenigo, the Papal Nuncio to Germany during the Second World War. The article discussed his failure to help the Jews. He'd died, conveniently, in April 1946. She didn't see his name again in the diary. There were only a few more entries before the final one, the one they had assumed was a suicide note.

A chill had entered the room. She'd never noticed Orsenigo's name before. Or perhaps she'd seen it, but there hadn't been any reason to check who he was. She stood, rubbed her arms. She felt light-headed. She would have to start cooking dinner soon. Alek would be hungry. She couldn't leave him to watch TV alone much longer. She turned and gripped the edge of the wooden bookcase as she exited the room.

This was just what she needed. Why did this have to happen when Sean was away? Memories of her father shouting, falling down, came to her. He'd been an embarrassment for such a long time. She'd never thought too much about why he'd been that way, about why he drank. It had just been a given, like wet summers and cold winter walks to school.

How did her family story connect with the letter she'd been shown by Fred Corbett? Had the Catholic hierarchy secretly supported Hitler? Was that what had upset her Grandfather so much, that he had killed himself? Had the Vatican managed to hide this ever since?

She went down the stairs, holding the banisters tight, pushing memories away. She checked the front door, slid the upper and lower bolts across, then headed to the kitchen. She peered out into the garden, at their back wall topped with razor spikes. She felt unsettled, as if danger lurked somewhere out there. Had Fred been right about people looking for him?

She shook her head. No, the Catholic Church was not a force for evil. Maybe they'd made mistakes in the past, but that was long ago. They didn't murder people who threatened to expose them. Did they?

She bit her lip.

She hadn't taken much interest in religion herself since she was a child. It had been frowned on in her house. Her father had overheard her talking on the phone to a boy from a Catholic school once, who wanted her to go to Mass with him. He'd shaken his head at her. Logic and reason had been his path, emotions always suppressed, unless he was drunk. That was the way he survived. She'd picked a lot up from him. If she hadn't met Sean she'd probably be drinking like an idiot still too, like she used to in college.

She checked the back door was locked for a second time, pulled the blind down over the window. Then she went to the small silver screen on the kitchen wall. It showed a live feed from a security camera at the front of the house.

She picked up the phone nearby. Rose, her friend from across the street, was waiting for her call. Rose had also spent money installing security equipment in the last few years. Between the two of them, their surveillance cameras covered most of the street.

The first thing Isabel would ask her friend would be if she had seen anything suspicious. She held the phone in her hand, her fingers poised above the keys. Her knuckles were white. No, she couldn't say that. Rose would think something was wrong. She'd probably drop the phone in fright.

She wouldn't call Rose. She would call Sean. She had to talk to him. She stared at the phone. She'd put his mobile number on speed dial, but which button had she put it on? Her mind was numb, frozen. Memories of her father arguing, drunkenly, about religion with her mother had come flooding in. She hadn't thought about those fights in years.

She jumped. The phone was ringing. The noise echoed around the kitchen.

"Yes."

"Henry Mowlam, Mrs Ryan. I have an answer to the question you asked me yesterday."

When she'd seen the two gurneys being taken out to an ambulance at the hotel the night before, she hadn't been able to make out who was on them. She's called Henry when she got home. She'd left a message on his voicemail.

"Henry, good to hear from you." She paused, wondered did she sound too eager. But it really was good to hear a friendly voice. There was silence for a few more seconds, as if Henry was deciding how to respond.

"Before I tell you, you must promise me one thing."

"What?"

"That you will not get involved in investigating these deaths."

She pressed her lips together to stop herself exploding. She spoke slowly, when the words came out.

"You'll have to tell me who died before I can promise you anything." She knew what his answer would be, but still she had to hear the words.

"No. I want your promise first, Mrs Ryan." He said it in such a clipped manner, she knew he wasn't going to bend.

The call would be over in the next minute if she made the wrong decision.

"Okay, Henry. I will not get involved in investigating these deaths." She waited. Seconds ticked by.

"The people you went to meet for InfoFreed died within minutes of your meeting. A police interview will be arranged with you over the next few days."

His confirmation made a sickening hollow open up inside her. She bent at the waist, as the reality of what had happened to Fred and Daisy sank in.

"Oh my God, Henry." She was almost whispering.

"That isn't all I'm going to tell you, Mrs Ryan, now that I have your promise."

"Go on." What else would he say? Wild thoughts flashed.

"The pictures you spoke about in your voice message were recovered at the scene. We must ask you not to discuss them with anyone. We believe the letter in the pictures is a fake. Our analysis will confirm that."

"You've pre-ordained the outcome?" She tried not to sound shocked, but couldn't. His conclusion about the letter had to be premature. What was going on?

24

June 23ʳᵈ 1940

The two hundred and ten horsepower Mercedes 770 touring limousine purred to a stop on the cobbled drive of the Parvis du Sacré-Cœur in Paris.

Two Zündapp Wehrmacht sidecar motorcycles had already pulled up ahead. The SS men who had been riding them were standing with their black MP-38 machine pistols held in front of them, sweeping the area from side to side, covering the steps up to the white basilica of Sacré-Cœur as well as the street leading back down towards the centre of the city.

Two other Zündapp sidecar motorcycles pulled up behind the car. They blocked access to the street in front of Sacré-Cœur, the iconic Catholic basilica on the highest point in Paris. The engine of the Mercedes limousine remained on and the blackened windows closed. A steady exhaust stream emanated from the tailpipe. It was another minute before a door opened.

The two men who stepped from the back of the vehicle wore glistening leather trench coats and SS caps. They turned, surveyed the scene, then tapped on the front window of the vehicle. It was a warm morning. Sunlight streamed over the gray slate roofs of the city below.

In the distance the top of the Arc de Triomphe and the Eiffel Tower were visible, though not the giant black and red Swastika that hung in the centre of the Arc de Triomphe. A musty smell hung in the air, though it wasn't from any damage the city had suffered, it was the smell of Paris, tinged with a whiff of garbage, as rubbish collections had been reduced to almost zero, due to a lack of manpower in the last few weeks.

The city had been occupied nine days before. The night curfew that the victorious Gestapo had imposed meant that few civilians were around at eight thirty that morning.

Standing at the top of the steps was a small welcoming committee. Three men in long black cassocks, two of whom wore violet skull caps, stood in front of the open main doors of Sacré-Cœur, which gleamed white above them, its main cupola raising high into the air.

This was the last, and most important stop on the victor's tour of Paris. The small group of four, Hitler, an SS Lieutenant, Albert Speer, and General Speidel, took the steps slowly. They turned twice to take in the view of Paris below the hill of Montmartre.

When they reached the triple height bronze doors Speer pointed up at one of the statues above.

"Joan of Arc, Mein Führer. She awaits," he said, in German, his excitement clear from his voice.

Hitler didn't look up. He strode towards the three clerics who stood waiting for him. Each man had his arm raised in the Nazi salute.

"Sieg Heil," they said, respectfully, as the Führer approached.

Hitler returned the salute. He shook hands with each man.

"A blessed victory has been granted us, Mein Führer," said Nuncio Orsenigo, in German. He bowed his head, as he shook the Führer's hand. Hitler pulled his hand away quickly, though whether it was to hide the slight tremble that afflicted him that morning, or out of distaste for Orsenigo, it was hard to tell.

"Show us our spoils, Orsenigo," he said. He squeezed the Nuncio's arm as they walked through the doors.

Orsenigo waved at the view in front of them, as if offering the great basilica to Hitler.

Hitler's smile was thin, but his eyes were wide, as if savoring a feast. "You got here quicker than me, Orsenigo. Your job in the Fatherland is perhaps not enough for you?"

"I am blessed with my position, Mein Führer. I thank the Lord every day for allowing me to carry out my duties." Orsenigo leaned close to Hitler as they walked through the doors. He pointed forward toward the apse, where the gloom of the nave was brightened by a row of tall candles. The candlelight reflected onto the giant mosaic which filled the curved wall high above the altar. The mosaic glistened with gold. At its centre, Jesus' arms were outstretched against a sky blue background.

"Our Lord approves of your conquest." He stopped at the first row of wooden pews, looked up at the mosaic, put his hands together, as if in prayer. The pews had been empty all the way up to the altar. The only other person that could be seen was an old bald priest standing to the right of the main altar, which was above the level of the rest of the church, beyond wide stone steps.

"Do you know the will of God, Orsenigo?" said Hitler. He turned, taking in the rows of tree trunk-like stone pillars running up the basilica on each side. Nearby, Speer was talking excitedly to Speidel in a low voice. His words, in German, fell into the hushed interior of the basilica like heavy stones dropping into a smooth pond.

Hitler breathed deep, closed his eyes. Lingering smells of incense and candle wax drifted in the air.

"Come, let us talk about the will of God, Mein Führer." Orsenigo was leaning close again, as if his words were only meant for Hitler.

He walked away, looking back only once to check that Hitler and his entourage were behind him.

The sound of leather soles slapping hard on the pale mosaic floor made the priest who had been watching them step back, in fear. Orsenigo went straight past the man without even a nod in his direction. Behind Hitler, one of the other two men in cassocks paused briefly and whispered something in French to the priest. The priest blessed himself and walked fast towards the bronze main doors.

Cesare Orsenigo, Papal Nuncio, the Vatican's Ambassador to Berlin, approached the side of the main altar

Laurence O'Bryan

and pushed open a door in the bronze lattice screen. It separated the altar from the main body of the church. As it creaked on its hinges Orsenigo stepped through.

Hitler followed without hesitation. Then the two other churchmen passed through. After they had done so, the last priest, a tall man with a long aquiline nose and skin as thin and gray as his hair, turned and raised his hand to stop Speer and the others in Hitler's party following.

"We will look after the Führer from here," said the priest, in a soothing voice.

Hitler turned and watched as Speer hesitated at the other side of the door.

"Wait here," said Hitler. He slid his hand across his forehead, pushing a stray hair into place. He rose up a little on his toes as he continued, his accent strident now.

"If I don't return in thirty minutes, you have my direct order to burn this place, and every other Catholic cathedral in the Reich to the ground, and then take every blackened nail and candlestick and melt them down in a furnace to make bullets for the Fatherland. Understood?"

Speer gave the Nazi salute.

The gray-faced priest stared at Hitler, as if he'd cursed them all.

Orsenigo stepped forward.

"Nuncio Valerie will stay outside with your colleagues, Mein Führer." He bowed, then waved at the third prelate. This man had hair which was oiled to his scalp, round glasses and a prominent chin. He stepped back through the bronze lattice-work door and pulled it closed with a click, as if he

134

was long used to taking orders and responding promptly, no matter what he was asked to do.

"Follow me, Mein Führer," said Orsenigo. They passed a row of thick candles. Orsenigo turned and went to the side of the carved stone altar-piece, though it seemed as if there was no place for him to go. Hitler watched as Orsenigo pressed a small square stone carving on the back wall. The wall behind it moved. A low roofed passage became visible behind the altar.

"Another church of secret places," said Hitler. "I should have guessed."

Orsenigo didn't reply. The sound of footsteps disappearing could be heard as Hitler approached the hidden door. He looked behind before going through. The altar screen blocked any view of the rest of the church at ground level. He felt for his silver-handled Walther PP pistol in the polished leather holster under his coat. He loosened his coat buttons, headed down the circular stone stairs. The walls were white, like the stone of the basilica up above, but after two turns the stone turned darker, rougher.

"Another of your ceremonies, is that what you have up your sleeve?" said Hitler, loudly. Thick yellow bulbs lit up the stairs, but as they were set widely apart, there was a deep gloom in the stairwell in places.

"I want to show you the oldest part of our sacred Church, Mein Führer. It originates from before the Benedictine nuns took over the site a thousand years ago. There is something important I want you to see," Orsenigo replied, his voice drifting up from below.

They kept going down.

There was a dank smell now. Hitler sniffed, then patted his moustache down, as if a nervous tick had struck him. They reached a small room at the bottom of the stairs. The walls were made of stone slates piled on top of each other, ancient brickwork. Orsenigo passed through a narrow door opposite the bottom of the stairs. Hitler followed.

The underground room they entered was laid out as a small chapel. There was a small altar, made of pale green marble at the far end, and stone pews, for people to rest their knees on, in rows in front of it. There were no seats. At the back of the altar was a large gold tabernacle, with a face, with closed eyes embossed thickly on it. A row of yellow electric bulbs hung from each wall. They flickered occasionally.

"What is this place?" said Hitler.

"Mein Führer, this is the first Christian prayer room built on Montmartre. It was crafted by the followers of St. Denis, more than fourteen hundred years ago," said Orsenigo.

Hitler walked towards the corbelled wall. It curved, beehive-like, towards a point in the roof. He put his hand out, touched the wall, as if he was stroking a cat.

"This reminds me of the old Germanic tombs we find in the Black Forest."

"It has been in continuous use from 357A.D., when the Roman Emperor Julian visited here. He wanted to unify the empire, as you want to unify Europe today." Orsenigo smiled. "He was told that if he kneeled and prayed to his Saviour, his wish would be granted."

"Julian failed, Orsenigo. Can I assume from that, that he refused to kneel?"

Orsenigo shrugged, as if the answer was obvious. "The city above was saved from Attila the Hun by prayers at this wall," he said, pointing at the wall behind the altar. "Your visit to Paris is doubly blessed by coming down here to this holy place, Mein Führer. We have prayed for your victory here. We have appealed to all the saints and to all the archangels, that your victory would be swift, and that His peace will once more reign, under your guidance."

Hitler walked towards the tabernacle.

Orsenigo put his hand out, as if to prevent Hitler touching it. Then he blessed himself. "Mein Führer, I will show you everything, but in a moment."

"Good, but let it be clear." Hitler's tone was angry. "I am not here to worship relics, Orsenigo. You said you wanted to discuss how we can work together in France if I came here." He rocked on his heels, a questioning look on his face. Then he pushed his hair across his forehead again, flattening it into place with his hand.

Orsenigo bowed, deeply. "You will have our support from every pulpit, in every church in France for your new regime here, Mein Führer. This is what we offer."

Hitler sniffed, paused, made Orsenigo wait for his reply. "And in recognition of this, the Catholic church will take its rightful place back at the heart of French life, as it does in the Fatherland. This is agreed."

Orsenigo nodded, took a gold key from the deep side pocket of his cassock. He walked forward, then leaned to the centre of the altar, put the key into the tabernacle and opened it. It spilt apart, the two doors folding noiselessly to the side. The temperature in the room dropped. Orsenigo turned and motioned Hitler forward to see what was inside the tabernacle. Hitler came up behind Orsenigo, then took a step back, surprised by what he saw.

There was an opening at the back of the tabernacle, beyond a thin shelf. The opening was about two-foot square, big enough to slide through, if you were a child or a small young man. On the shelf inside the tabernacle was a letter in a white envelope, edged with yellow. Beyond the shelf he could dimly make out a large space, and bones, lots of gray bones, all small or medium sized, and stacked up, all the femurs and tibias and fibulas and small skulls together, piled up against the far wall.

It looked as if a charnel house had been emptied into the space behind the wall and someone had arranged every bone with meticulous care.

"Martyrs, Orsenigo?" said Hitler.

"They all died for their faith, Mein Führer." He blessed himself, then handed Hitler the letter with the yellow edge.

Hitler turned it over. On the front, Adolf Hitler, Führer, was written in a large florid script.

"I hope this is what I expect, Orsenigo." He ripped the letter open, breaking a gold wax seal on the back. It had a crown and keys embedded on it. A piece of the seal fell to the floor.

Hitler took a sheet of thin yellow paper from inside the envelope. He read what was written on it, then slapped the paper with the back of his hand.

"Tell the Holy Father that my answer is yes."

Orsenigo blessed himself, faced the tabernacle, chin up, then turned to Hitler.

"We pray only for your victory, and for the Fatherland's, Mein Führer." He bowed.

Hitler nodded, then looked at the letter in his hand again. He licked his lips. His eyes were bulging.

"Assure the Holy Father that Russia will be subjugated within one year." He pointed at Orsenigo. "I will keep my word. The communists will not know what hit them."

He put the letter in the inside pocket of his coat.

"But I expect absolute support from every priest in every town in every country where we rule." His voice rose. "The Fatherland demands it, Orsenigo." Spittle flew from his mouth. He was pointing at Orsenigo now. "Never, ever forget it. We take each stop together."

"You will receive our support, Führer. The will of God our Father and all the angels and saints will be done through you." Orsenigo raised his arm, blessing Hitler again.

Hitler brushed his hair to the side. His hand was trembling.

"The whole world needs us, Orsenigo," said Hitler. "Europe will be overrun with Jews and communists without us."

He went to the tabernacle, looked through it at the bones. "Whose bones are those? They look new."

Orsenigo came up beside him and whispered in his ear. "This is the other matter we need to discuss."

25

"What do you mean, he's dead?" Bile rose in Sean's throat.

"I don't mean to alarm you, Herr Ryan."

"Someone murdered him? But why?"

"We cannot be sure." Kurt shrugged.

"How do you know?"

"His body was dumped in the Pegnitz River. He had a bullet wound in his forehead. It appears to be a professional job."

"What the hell's happening in Germany?" Sean's voice shook. "This is the fascist era coming back."

Kurt sat upright in the hotel chair, stared straight at Sean.

"I can tell you one thing, for certain, Herr Ryan. There are a lot of German people who will stand against anything like that returning."

Sean bent his head, groaned. "But Jerome is dead. And Eleni too!" His voice cracked. He pressed his fist to his chest, bent forward. A strangled groan poured from his throat.

"My uncle was hanged by the Nazis in 1940," said Kurt, softly. "He was seventeen. His only crime was to speak out against them in beer halls here in Nuremberg. My grandfather was forced to help bury him. Then he was forced to join the Nazi party."

Sean looked at Kurt for a minute, the concept of burying your son in such circumstances sent a further twist into his gut. "You are right to be proud of your uncle."

"I think he would have spoken out now too." Kurt pursed his lips.

"There is a darkness in Germany again. If you are against refugees and people who are different, you get interviewed on TV and in the newspapers. Commentators don't challenge these people. Refugees are painted as demons, rapists. Hate is turning to violence everywhere."

"But why would anyone want to kill Jerome and Eleni?"

Kurt pointed at Sean. "Here in Bavaria we have a number of anti-refugee groups. One of them is called the 39 Boys. You can read about them on the internet. They are dangerous. Very dangerous. They stir up trouble so that right wing politicians will get elected. Every member of that group should have been put in prison a long time ago and their pay masters. I expect this group, or people like them, murdered your friends."

A shout echoed from the street below. Kurt went to the window, looked down.

"Punks."

"If you know who the people in this group are, are your colleagues going around knocking on their doors, arresting them?"

"It's not that easy."

"That's bullshit. You're not even questioning them? But you're interviewing family members as if they're guilty. What the hell is that about?"

Kurt opened his mouth, hesitated. Then he leaned forward. "What I will tell you must not be repeated, Herr Ryan, understood?"

Sean nodded.

Kurt sounded angry, when he continued. "We had a security breach at the national police computer system a few months ago. All records of the 39 Boys and two other anti-refugee groups were deleted." He sat back.

"What about backups?" Sean's tone was angry.

"Everything is gone. Every file. Every backup. I only found this out when I tried to check on a suspect. There wasn't even an official announcement about the security breach." He shook his head slowly, an amazed look on his face.

"That's incredible. How could this be allowed to happen?" Sean shifted in his chair.

"I reported my concerns to a member of the Landtag of Bavaria. To someone who sits on the Committee of National Security."

"You trust politicians?"

"This one, yes. She holds people to account. She is one of the good guys, isn't that how you say it? I'm doing my best, Herr Ryan, but things are moving fast." He pointed at the TV. "Have you been watching the news?"

"A little."

"CXN Deutschland have been covering something, which you should see." He picked up the TV remote from the bed, flicked through the channels. "Ja." He'd found CXN.

On the screen a young woman with swept back blond hair was standing outside a modern 3-storey building talking fast in German, an ambulance with a strobing blue light flashing behind her, sending pulses of blue through her hair.

"What's she saying?" Another ambulance pulled up.

"There's been an outbreak of some unidentified disease. Twenty-six refugees have died in Nuremberg in the past twelve hours. Two in Munich."

Sean was trying to work out the words that were moving across the bottom of the screen. All he recognised was a number – 31.

He pointed. "Are there 31 people dead now?" His skin pricked. Was there a connection between Jerome and Eleni's murders and this? Was that what Kurt was implying?

"Ja, that is the death toll now."

"Something's spreading among refugees?"

The prickling on his skin grew warmer. Someone had planned to infect a demonstration with a virus in London a few years before. Hatred had inspired that sickening attempt. He thought about Isabel and Alek back in London. He was glad they were there, not here. Any member of the public could be an enemy, a soft target, these days.

Kurt bent his head, as if something was weighing down on him.

"What do you make of all this?" Sean spoke fast, waved at the screen.

Kurt replied quickly. "All the people who have died so far are from north Africa, Herr Ryan. I don't like that."

Sean let out a snort. "It's a coincidence. It has to be. There couldn't be a virus that just infects one group." His voice rose. He lifted his hand, pressed his palm to his forehead.

"You think someone is trying to infect refugees?" He put his hand down, gripped the edge of the chair.

Kurt didn't respond. They started at each other.

"You think someone has developed a way of infecting just one group they want eliminated?"

Kurt pointed at the screen. "It has to be a possibility for these deaths. We have to consider it." The outside broadcast had been replaced by a studio shot of a white-coated doctor, captioned, *Doktor Oskar Strausse.*

"Be quiet, please." Kurt put his hand up to stop Sean talking.

He listened, shook his head, slowly.

"I don't believe it."

"What?"

"This doctor says all these deaths are likely to be caused by a viral infection brought in to Germany by refugees. He's talking about the need for secure camps to separate possible carriers."

"That's going to spread panic," said Sean. "Do you think this is connected to Jerome and Eleni?"

"Your friend Jerome was about to publish an academic paper on genetically matched medicine. Did you know that?"

"I heard about it. Eleni was afraid he'd never get it published if they moved. You think that's got something to do with this?" He waved at the TV.

"A pharmaceutical company is doing this type of research here in Nuremberg, Herr Ryan."

"You think they're involved?" The idea was crazy. If such research got into the wrong hands, racists on every continent would be interested it. There could be mass slaughter.

Kurt spoke softly now. "I don't know. Perhaps this is simply an accident. A worker at the research facility may have broken their protocols." He stood, looked out the window.

"What's the name of this company?"

"Nufaben. Their research laboratory is a few miles from here."

"Have you investigated this place?"

"No, I have had no reason to."

"How do you know what they do?"

"A cousin of mine works there. She says they operate seven days a week. Their security is the tightest she has ever seen."

"Are your colleagues blaming Nufaben?"

"No. People are blaming an imported virus."

"I'd like to see this facility."

"I thought you might say that." Kurt put his hand in the pocket of his black three-quarter-length jacket. He seemed to be looking for something.

26

Henry Mowlam, duty officer for MI5's central London monitoring desk, was on weekend duty. It was a full working day for him that Sunday. There had been a number of incidents. An ISIS-affiliated terror suspect, who had been questioned the previous day, had given details of a plot to attack a night club in central London. He had only cooperated after his decrypted online messages had been shown to him. Arrests were taking place as a result.

But something else had caught Henry's attention in the last few minutes. A demonstration had begun in front of the German embassy in Belgrave Square in the city centre.

He logged on to the live link with the MI5 video link screen. He could see and hear what was going on, as if he was standing over the crowd. Many demonstrators carried placards in Arabic and English saying WHO IS KILLING US? There were other messages too. A woman in a hijab, which covered her hair, was carrying a black flag. She was shouting something in Arabic. He clicked a key to take a picture of her, then fed it into the database. She came up as a Syrian refugee seeking long-term residency in the United

Kingdom, because a sibling had already been granted it. She was also associated with a mosque on his watch list.

"Foolish," he murmured. He gathered still images of several other demonstrators and got similar results.

He ran a wider network search. All the people he'd selected were also family members of people who had died in the German virus outbreak.

He lifted the phone. "Take a look at the Belgrave Square news feed. Translate audio please."

"Okay."

The translator did her job quickly. Text came up at the bottom of the video. What sounded like shouted slogans in English and Arabic were mostly the same message: "Get our families out of Germany. God is great."

The question all this raised was: why were so many people of a similar origin dying in Germany? And if, as MI6 had suggested, there was an infection loose among the refugee community there, what would be the impact on the United Kingdom, with its large refugee population, particularly in London?

Henry leaned towards the screen. He read a briefing note from an MI6 officer in Munich. It had popped into a corner. *The situation in Bavaria is of serious concern at this time. A move by the Bundespolizei to place the city of Nürenberg under quarantine will be passed to the Federal Ministry of Health (Bundesministerium für Gesundheit) for an emergency session, late today, Sunday. Of immediate UK concern, is the escalating number of casualties (43 at this time), the number of victims hospitalised, and the likelihood*

*that infected individuals may have already boarded flights
to the United Kingdom. ID/passport numbers of all those
infected are provided in the attached list.*

Henry scanned the list, then emailed it to the Border
Agency duty officer. He would have to make the decision to
escalate and request that the United Kingdom Health
Defence Committee be convened.

He turned to the second screen on his desk. It was
scrolling through a series of messages from the Metropolitan
Police concerning the incident at the German Embassy. He
composed a message to the duty officer.

Incident File 65876/876334/A

*I recommend a chemical incident unit, and arrest units,
be deployed at this time for the protection of the German
Embassy/London and the security of the United Kingdom.
Emergency Quarantine Directive HM765745/3 applies to
this incident.*

He sat back before pressing the send icon. His chair
squeaked. The forced detention and quarantine of
individuals, and the deprivation of all normal rights of
movement, travel and association was a serious matter, for
which he would have to account in full within hours.

He pressed the send button, then began saving the files he
had been looking at earlier, reports of racist incidents and
recent deaths in the Federal Republic of Germany. As he
saved them he was struck by the fact that there were so many
to choose from.

How many years had it been since such a broad range of racially motivated attacks had taken place in Germany? Major Finch would be interested in all this.

The red telephone on his desk warbled. He picked it up.

"Yes, Major Finch," he said. He smiled to himself.

"What the hell's going on, Mowlam? I've just had a call from the Prime Minister's office."

27

Sean took the face mask that was being held out towards him. It was made of see-through plastic.

"You think we're in danger?

"No, but let's be prepared." Kurt patted his jacket pocket. "I have another one."

He pointed at Sean. "If I'm asked, I'm simply showing you where this factory is."

Only in Germany, thought Sean, would you get away with visiting a factory as a Sunday afternoon outing.

"Can you call in to see if there's been any progress on finding Jerome?"

Kurt didn't reply, but when they were on the street he took out his phone, made a call and spent a few minutes asking rapid-fire questions. When he was finished, he turned to Sean.

"Very little has been done on the investigation of your friend's disappearance. Most of our personnel are helping out at the hospitals or enforcing a quarantine order on the relatives of those who are dying in the outbreak. The numbers are increasing. I will have to go in and join my colleagues as soon as I get back."

There were few people on the street.

"Where is everybody? The city feels deserted."

"I believe people will be at home mostly, watching TV or following the situation at the hospitals online."

Sean shivered. A cold wind was blowing. Its gusts carried an icy edge from Siberia.

"Why are you taking me to this factory?"

"You will understand when we get there," said Kurt. He stopped at a black Audi A6. It had darkened windows and a silver line down the side.

"Your undercover car?" said Sean.

"My partner's vehicle," said Kurt.

Fifteen minutes later, after passing through the centre of the city, then heading east, they arrived at the edge of a modern industrial estate. There was a plan of the estate below the word *Gewerbegebiet* on a bulky plastic noticeboard. It looked as if it could withstand a snowstorm.

Kurt pulled up beside it.

"That part," he pointed at a section of the map shaded in green, "is where Nufaben have their headquarters. The whole area has high security. The best place to see the facility is from the end of this road." He pointed ahead. In the distance the road went straight to a dead end.

The road ended in a square concrete open area, where vehicles could turn. There was a wire mesh blocking access to fields of stunted grass on three sides, where buildings had yet to be put up. The place had an air of unfinished business.

Kurt rolled the car to the edge of the roadway, pointed down to the left, where the ground fell away, and the roof of a large industrial building could be seen in the distance. Beyond the building, there was a wood of tall, thin trees. The building was in the shape of a square.

He turned to Sean. "I suggest you get some pictures."

Sean didn't answer. He opened the door, went over to the fence and stared down at the factory. He used his phone and snapped the buildings below them. A thin wisp of smoke emanated from a stubby black chimney in one corner.

28

The smart phone lying on Vanessa Sheer's bed buzzed. She had been preparing an email for the heads of all divisions within the bank. Ensuring a calm reaction to whatever happened to the financial markets on Monday was essential.

Xena was on the other end of the line.

"Where will we meet?" Her tone was abrupt.

"I've been waiting for your call."

There was a hesitation at the other end.

"I was busy."

"Meet me at the Nufaben facility in one hour. I will send you a map. You are still in Nuremberg?"

"Yes."

She copied a map into the secure message app, then pressed the end call button. Then she pressed the message self-destruct button. The image that had been sent to Xena would delete itself in thirty seconds.

She stood, began texting on the encrypted messaging system. There could be no mistakes at this point. All the loose ends had to be tied up properly.

29

"That smoke will be from the heating system." Kurt was standing beside Sean.

"Are those guard posts?" There were two small concrete buildings below the perimeter fence, half way down to the other buildings.

"Yes, but most of the security is electronic these days. Perimeter sensors will tell the security manager within half a second if anyone, or anything, comes within ten metres of the facility, perhaps less."

"What are those rows of buildings?" To the right, beyond the perimeter fence of the compound, were rows of long, single story, flat roofed buildings. There were four rows of five buildings.

"Those were built for gastarbeiters, guest workers. There are mostly Syrians living there now. Two hundred can live in each building. The rooms inside hold four people, so families can be reunited. They don't mix Syrians with the Afghanis or the Libyans any more. Too many fights. Most of the men work in the factory on low-level duties or in other factories nearby. They get minimum wages and are discouraged from joining our unions. This is what the riots are really about."

One of the furthest buildings, near the road, was a blackened shell.

"What happened there," said Sean.

"The reception building for refuges was burnt down a few weeks ago. It hasn't been rebuilt. Nufaben tell us the camp is full and that all health and safety regulations are adhered to. But the security company that guards the camp failed to report the fire for thirty minutes. The building could not be saved by the time the fire trucks got here."

"But there are half-built blocks?"

"Yes, but it's unlikely the camp will take any more refugees."

"I've seen enough." Sean headed back to the car.

As Kurt drove slowly out of the estate, he glanced at Sean. "You will be able to identify the buildings from satellite images?"

Sean didn't reply.

"I did my research Herr Ryan. You wrote a paper about patterns in satellite images." He slowed as he turned a corner. "You identified unmarked Nazi era mass graves near Munich. This means you have access to the best satellite imaging systems."

Sean kept staring straight ahead. So that was why Kurt had suggested coming. He wanted people outside Germany to know what was happening here. The U.S. National Reconnaissance Office Lacrosse satellite, which crossed over Western Europe every three hours, provided high resolution radar, optical, infrared and ultraviolet images to security cleared organisations. His institute was one of them.

The satellite weighed fifteen tons and orbited three hundred and ninety miles above the Earth's surface. Its potential for agriculture, urban planning, and tax gathering was enormous. It had other uses, too. Digital images permitted the generation of data to assess the number of people attending demonstrations for instance.

If he requested a series of images for the Nufaben buildings and the guest worker buildings, he would be able to track any changes to the facility over time and the location of similar building patterns.

"Drive me to their front gate."

"Why, Herr Ryan?"

"I'm going to ask them a question."

Kurt turned the car left at the next turn. Two minutes later they were at the front of the facility. He switched off the engine nodded towards the redbrick guardhouse, which watched over the high, wire mesh gate barring the road.

Kurt shrugged. "Go ahead."

Sean walked to a glass panel in the wall of the guardhouse. It opened as he came near. He couldn't see more than a shadow inside, but the voice, in German, that barked at him made it clear his presence was considered suspicious.

He looked inside the guard post. Two heavy set men, with graying crew cuts, were staring back at him, grim-faced.

"I am here to meet Jerome Ruzibiza. Can you tell him I've arrived, please?"

The two men looked at each other. One of them picked up a smart phone and started tapping. He pressed something, put the phone to his ear, listened, then, after about half a minute, he closed the line.

"He is not here." There was no suggestion to leave a message or come back later, but he'd found out what he wanted.

"You are finished?" said Kurt, when he got back in the car.

"Yes."

"I will drop you back into the city."

An urge to leave, to get away from the city immediately, came over Sean. He resisted it. He had to find out more about what had happened to Jerome and Eleni. He owed it to them. He shook his head. What the hell was it about this city that made him so uneasy?

He looked out the window as they passed the rows of guest worker buildings.

"Why did Hitler pick Nuremberg for his rallies?"

"It's the old capital city of the Holy Roman Empire. And his favorite church, the Frauenkirche, is here."

They had left the industrial estate behind and were held up at a traffic light as a tram crossed the road in front of them, clanking loudly.

"I didn't know he was Catholic."

Kurt turned and looked at Sean.

"That's how he was brought up. Some say he never left the church. They didn't kick him out. I heard he kept a picture of his mother by his bed until the end. She was

Catholic, too. You do know his first international treaty was with the Vatican."

"So that's why he had his early rallies outside the Frauenkirche?"

"I expect so. You know there's a curse attached to the Frauenkirche, Herr Ryan."

"What curse?"

"I was told the story when I was young. They say that if anyone disturbs the spirits there, the devil will suck them down into hell."

Sean shook his head. "Who believes in curses anymore?"

A clattering sounded from above.

"Look," said Kurt. Flying above the street, in formation, was a line of dark gray helicopters. There must have been ten of them.

Kurt slowed, stared. "They are here to enforce the quarantine zone and to transport victims." He sounded very matter-of-fact.

Cars beeped. Kurt started moving again.

"What a nightmare." Sean felt another urge to go to the airport, to leave Nuremberg to its troubles.

"This is the worst thing that has happened here in decades." Kurt paused, then continued. "The BfV will be here soon."

"Who?"

"Our domestic intelligence service. If you see a lot of men with sunglasses, you will know who they are."

"Surely, it can't be that easy to spot them."

"Believe me, it is."

They passed a set of high iron gates. Sean stared at them. They had a square symbol with what looked like an arrow inside it on the front of the gates.

"What's that place?" he said, turning as they went past.

"It's an old Nazi era orphanage. It's closed a long time."

The gates had thick chains locking them.

"They carried out human experiments there. It was covered up for decades."

"Bastards."

"Where will I drop you? At your hotel?"

"No, at the Frauenkirche. I'd like to see the dig going on there that Jerome told me about. He said there'd be a lot of bodies under it."

Kurt slowed for a traffic light. He turned to Sean. "I wish our history was different, Herr Ryan. In 1936 Hitler made a speech there, about the future being German, and that we'd been given the right to rule the world." He sighed.

"He was an evil fantasist."

"He knew how to press people to his will. He was a magician, Herr Ryan."

Kurt drove into a car park, stopped. There were notices around them about what was *verboten*.

"It was said for many years that his rise to power was a miracle. I think the German people wanted that miracle. And when the Catholic priests told their congregations, every Sunday, that it was their duty to follow their Führer, few argued." He pointed at a doorway in a high brick wall. It had a green sign with the word *Ausweg* on it. "I have to report for duty. If you take that door, you will be on the street leading to the Frauenkirche. What is your plan for later?" He looked at Sean, as if concerned for him.

"I might go to the end of conference dinner tonight," said Sean. As soon as the words came out of his mouth he knew it wasn't going to happen. He didn't want to have to lie about how he was feeling to anyone.

A loud knock sounded on the driver's window. Kurt turned fast. He had one hand on his waist. Sean saw the black mesh-patterned metal of a gun handle poking out from his waistband.

Kurt said something in German, jabbed a finger at a button on the door. The window rolled down.

He shouted something. A man's face appeared. He was about forty with dark slicked-back hair. He was in civilian clothes, jeans and a navy jacket, but Sean could see a gun on his hip, too.

The man said something in German. It seemed to annoy Kurt. He shook his head, rolled the window closed. The man stood there, bent down, looking into the car. He stared at Sean, a hard look on his face.

"Who the hell's that?" said Sean.

"He's a colleague."

A rap sounded on the roof of the car. Then the man walked off. Kurt slammed a fist into the steering wheel.

"Nice guy," said Sean.

"No, he is not."

Sean didn't reply. They sat in silence as Kurt sat, stared straight ahead.

"What did he want?" said Sean a minute later.

"He was telling me I am needed at once, Herr Ryan. That we have work to do." His words came out fast.

It seemed as if every chance he had of finding out what had happened to Eleni and Jerome was slipping away.

"Do you know what happened here at the end of the war?"

"No," said Sean.

"The Werewolf underground resistance against Allied occupation was formed here in Nuremberg."

"It's still in existence?"

"No, it's not, but you should know there's a long history of people who would like to bring back Nazi ideas here."

Kurt shifted in his seat. His unease with all that was going on was clear.

"What's all that got to do with what's happening now?"

Kurt leaned towards Sean.

"You must put the pieces together, Herr Ryan."

"What does that mean?"

Kurt stared out the window.

"My wife was a policewoman. She died a few years ago." His tone was somber.

"I am sorry."

Kurt nodded. He didn't look at Sean.

"The investigation into her death was not handled properly."

"What do you mean?"

"Files have gone missing." He looked at Sean. "What's happening now reminds me of that time."

"What do you mean?"

"In Eleni Kibre's diary there was a reminder to herself about an interview with a journalist."

"Did it say what she was going to talk about?"

Kurt spoke again, his voice getting stronger with each word. "She was going to talk about Nazi medical experiments, and how similar experiments were carried out after the war, and what companies were involved." He sighed. "Now I have work to do." He put his hand out. Sean shook it.

Five minutes later Sean was in a café. He needed a coffee. He wasn't able to eat though, despite not having eaten anything in many hours. His stomach muscles felt twisted. There were only two other people in the café aside from the proprietor and a person who looked like his daughter. Those two people were both tapping away at their smartphones. The proprietor was listening to a radio. It sounded as if the news was on. All Sean could hear was a droning German monotone.

He stared through the window at the cobbled pavement outside.

Why had Jerome and Eleni been murdered?

He checked his phone. He'd missed a text from Isabel.

Are you okay? it read.

All good, C U tomorrow, he replied.

A shout sounded from the back of the café. He turned. The proprietor was coming towards him.

"Aus," he shouted. "Alle aus." His hands were waving threateningly in the air.

30

Vanessa Sheer placed her key card against the door pad of the Kaiser Suite at the five star Nuremberg Emperors' hotel. Moments later she stepped into the bedroom. She slid her long leather coat from her shoulders, stepped out of her skirt. She checked the temperature control unit on the sleek silver panel near the door.

Twenty-two degrees. Warm enough for her to prepare, but not too warm for what was to come. The room had an Emperor size bed pushed up against the back wall, mirrors on each of the other walls and another large mirror above the bed.

Black silk sheets made the bed gleam. They had prepared the room exactly as instructed. Two black silk covered pillows waited at the top.

Thick white candles stood in a row on a side table. She took a silver cigarette lighter from her black leather pouch-bag and lit each candle in turn, then glanced at her watch. They would be here in fifteen minutes. She had to be quick.

She pulled her Louis Vuitton suitcase near the bed. From it she extracted a black silk bra decorated with black pearls, black silk stockings and knickers, cut high.

She put them on the bed. What would her banker and politician colleagues think if they knew what she was up to?

Nothing! They were all enslaved to something or other. She had the details of each board member's secret deviances hidden away, ready for use if they ever threatened her.

She put on the black satin bra, the black silk stockings, fastened the suspenders to the stockings. From the suitcase she took a leather whip with knotted cords drooping from it, each tipped with a glistening shard of silver.

Holding the whip, she knelt, bowed her forehead, kissed a square-shaped cross embedded in silver, which she then placed back in the suitcase.

She stood after a few seconds and looked around. Each of the hundreds of pieces of glass in the chandelier twinkled as they reflected the light from the candles.

She went to the side table, picked up a tall Waterford crystal wine glass at the far end. Two drops fell into it from a small black bottle in her hand. They disappeared quickly into the red wine she poured from a bottle already opened nearby. She swallowed the concoction in one gulp. Soon her boys would arrive.

There would be three of them tonight. A tremble of anticipation passed through her. She caressed the whip.

A knock sounded from the other room. She pressed a switch. A moment later the door opened. Three six foot, blond males entered. They each looked no more than nineteen or twenty. They undressed as she watched. Each of their bodies glistened with muscular energy. To them she was a rich woman who wanted to play games.

Laurence O'Bryan

Each of them would follow her orders precisely. That was the way she liked it. They lined up for her to examine them. She fondled each of them. They grew bigger quickly. Soon, they were all smiling. Tingles slid up her arms and down her back. She gave an order. They knelt. Her whip crackled in the air. Each felt it in his turn. Not one of them grimaced. But two of them made their hands into fists after their turn came, and their eyes blazed.

They would be fired up properly now. She lay on the bed and motioned them to her, one after the other. As the cleansing power of their energy enveloped her she smiled, at last.

As the final moment approached, she let out a scream.

"Mein Gott, stop!"

The three of them pulled back together as if they had been slapped. Each of them was breathing heavily.

In a soft, girlish German, she said, "Put on those collars." She pointed at the black table. The three boys returned seconds later. Each of them was wearing a black priest's collar with white at the front. Her eyes widened, as memories flooded every cell of her brain.

Her naked body rose in the air as she was picked up on either side and the largest of the boys came towards her, grinning.

31

This was the right time to visit the Frauenkirche. He'd seen it when he'd visited the market square on Friday night, but he hadn't gone inside. He stopped and stared. Its roof was steep. Ornamental gothic spikes stood out against the gray clouds, and dark stained glass windows looked out over the cobbled square.

It was four in the afternoon. There were few people about. Most of them seemed to be hurrying somewhere.

As he crossed the square there were five or six market stalls still open in front of the Frauenkirche. They were selling wooden toys, jars of pickles and fruit to very few customers. He looked up at the Cathedral.

It wasn't as big St Paul's in London, but it was still imposing with its black and gray stone, medieval gargoyles and pale blue statues beneath the blue clock high up in its front wall. The main statue was of a man with a beard and gold crown, a depiction of the Holy Roman Emperor Charles V, so his guide app said.

It also said that the church had been built over the site of a synagogue, which had been destroyed during a pogrom against Jews in 1349. Apparently, they'd been blamed for bringing the Black Death to the city. The local elite had owed money to Jewish moneylenders, and had presumably come to the conclusion that mass murder was preferable to paying it back.

Sean walked around the church. There was no work going on at the site. Had Jerome been mistaken, or was the dig over?

He went back across the market square, to the nearest stall. It was laden with jars of fruit of various sizes. He examined a small jar of pears in thick juice. The woman selling the fruit was heavy-set and wearing a padded jacket. He asked her, in English, if there was archaeological work going on at the Frauenkirche recently. He pointed at the church. The woman shook her head slowly, shrugged. Then she pointed at one of the other stalls.

"Ich spreche kein Englisch. Sprechen sie mit ihm," she said. She smiled and waved him towards a man at the wooden toy stall nearby.

Sean went through the same procedure at the next stall. He examined a wooden medieval soldier, painted in blue and gold like the statues above them on the church, then asked the man the same question.

He shook his head. "No, there is none of this work going on there in the last year." His accent had a touch of American in it.

"A friend of mine said there was a dig here."

The man shook his head. "No, he must be mistaken. No digging up the past here recently, definitely not. We have enough problems, yes."

Sean was about to walk away, but a reply came to him.

"Was this church built on the site of a Jewish ghetto?"

"I don't know about that."

"I read that the synagogue was burnt down while hundreds of Jews were inside."

The man's face hardened. "The way I heard it, the Jews brought the Black Death here, which killed thousands."

"So they deserved to die?"

The stallholder shook his head. "I do not know the answer to that. I was not there."

Sean walked on, then consulted his guide app again, flicking past images of sights to see in Nuremberg. Maybe Jerome had confused the Frauenkirche with another church. He saw a picture of a church called St Laurence's and another with no roof, whitewashed walls and people praying inside. It was an odd image. It looked as if the building had been destroyed and never rebuilt. He found another stall holder who spoke English.

"Where are these churches?" He pointed at the two pictures on the screen.

"They are five minutes' walk from here. That way for St Catherine's." The woman pointed to the left, over the roof of the buildings at the far end of the square. "And this way for St Laurence's." She pointed over her shoulder.

"Is there archaeological work going on at any of these churches?"

"Ja. There is a big project going on at St Catherine's. They will finish it by summer, I hope. We can have our concerts again."

"Danke," he said.

He walked fast in the direction of St Catherine's. There were still a few hours to sunset, but the sun was nowhere to be seen. Gray clouds, rolling in from the east in thick blankets, obscured the sky and created an oppressive Sunday afternoon atmosphere, as if the whole world was waiting for Monday morning. His feelings matched the sky.

He'd been looking forward to coming here, but everything about the visit had turned to dust. Not only was an old friend dead, her partner was too. And he had no idea why. Memories of other deaths came back to him.

Too many.

The only thought that reassured him was that Isabel and Alek were safe. They had been through too much because of him already.

Perhaps he should let it all go, just go back to London. Try to forget.

As he walked down a narrow lane leading towards St Catherine's, in the oldest part of the city he'd been in so far, he remembered the injuries Eleni had suffered. The thought of what she must have gone through made a rage spill up inside him. How could anyone do that to another human?

When he reached the church he walked slowly around St Catherine's walls. The building was all locked up. He checked the chains on the ancient-looking barred gate set into a side wall. It faced into a narrow passage between medieval stone buildings. He'd read in the guide that St Catherine's had been the main church of Nuremberg in the seventeenth and eighteenth centuries, when it had been home to the Nuremberg Meistersingers. Wagner had created an opera during that era in Nuremberg. Albrecht Durer had painted a triptych for the altar.

The church had been destroyed when the American army took Nuremberg in 1945, and it had been left as a ruin to remind people what had happened to the city.

At the back of the church there was an eight-foot-high wire fence, protecting the rear wall. Sean looked through a gap in the fence. There were piles of rubble in a line of blue skips set in a row against the wire.

As he passed them he looked between the skips. A man on a bicycle went by. He stared at Sean, as if he knew he was a foreigner. Scan turned, saw a glimmer of an electric light from between the skips, bent down, as if tying a shoelace, then peered forward to get a better look.

Could there be someone in there on a Sunday? No, wasn't it more likely the light was on for a reason, perhaps for security guards inside? He looked up and down the wire fence. There were no security cameras on top of it.

But there was a thin wire on the top of the fence. He knew immediately what that was. They had considered the same thing for their house in Chelsea. It was an electronic trip wire. If anyone tried to climb over it an alarm would be set off. There was no way to get over this fence, unless you were a pole vaulter.

The wire was trembling in the wind. The system was probably capable of distinguishing between the weight of the wind or a sparrow, and a human, so that the alarm only went off when there really was a security incident underway.

He passed another skip. Light was coming from a window beyond it. It appeared to be part of a basement level. He stopped, leaned forward, careful not to touch the fence.

The gap between the skips only allowed him to see a part of the window, but the light inside it illuminated a stone passage wall beyond, with a curved ceiling. And there was something to the left that looked like the entrance to a staircase, as the roof curved down above it. The wall there was blackened stone, which looked older than the church above.

A draft of wind pushed him in the back. He almost reached forward and held the wire mesh, but he didn't. He looked down though and that was when he saw the bottom of the wire was bent a little. Perhaps a dog had gone through that way. He leaned down. Yes, the wire was loose at the bottom. He pulled it up a few inches, waited. No alarm sounded. No one came.

He could get through, if he didn't mind putting his chest into the dirt.

But should he? He bent the broken edge of the wire up higher, waited some more. Perhaps the place was remotely monitored. Perhaps no one was here. He could go in, have a look around, then get out again quickly, even if he did set off an alarm. All he wanted to do was see what was going on. If all these skips were anything to go by, they had to be digging deep. He hesitated.

Maybe he should leave. There wasn't any evidence connecting this site to what had happened to his friends. Then he remembered what Eleni had said about sites in

Nuremberg she was interested in. She'd said there was a lot still to be uncovered in the city. Was this site what she was talking about?

He imagined what Eleni would have said, if she had been here. She'd have encouraged him to go in. She wouldn't have taken him down below the Nazi rally grounds if she didn't believe in pushing your luck.

He had to do this. It was the least he could do for her memory.

He pulled the wire up some more. It would take only a few seconds to slip under it. He glanced down the lane, one way, then the other. The lane was empty. A snatch of distant rock music came to him on the wind. He might not get another chance like this. And what would they do if they caught him, slap his wrist?

He'd be in and out in a few minutes.

He bent down, slid under the gap.

His jacket caught.

He shifted, undid it. Still no alarm sounded. He stood up on the far side, brushed dirt away, walked along the wall of the church.

There was nobody around. He reached the square window. Light was still shining from it. A pane of dirty glass separated him from a stone corridor. The spiral staircase was fully visible now. He walked further along the wall. There was a door ahead. He reached it.

It was made of dark brown wood, flecked with black and reinforced with battered bronze straps. It looked as old as the building. He reached for the handle, a pitted bronze ball, turned it and pushed at the door. It was locked.

Of course it was locked. He bent down. There was a small keyhole below the handle. He wasn't going to get in easily. He should have watched that lock picking video online.

He continued along the wall, looked up. At the corner of the building, there was scaffolding. It reached to roof level, if the church still had one. There wouldn't be much point in going up there. The building was a shell.

He put his head around the corner. That was when he heard a scuffling behind him, like a rat scrambling on a wall.

32

Isabel tried to sit still, for fear of disturbing Alek. He looked like an angel, the Superman duvet thrown aside, his eyelids fluttering now and then. She put her palm to his brow. He definitely still had a temperature, but it seemed less than it had been an hour ago.

She stood, looked at her watch. She'd come back to check on him in fifteen minutes. She headed down to the kitchen, looked outside. Everything in the garden was wet from the rain that had been pouring all afternoon. The apple tree looked sad, bedraggled. She looked at their Aga. There was nothing cooking on it. If Sean had been here, they'd have started their Sunday supper by now. Perhaps they'd be eating that new Italian pasta, with that new Sicilian sauce.

She went to their double door fridge, took out the bottle of Chardonnay, unfinished from the night before, undid the cap, which was supposed to keep it drinkable, sniffed at the bottle, then poured the remains into the sink. The Sunday paper caught her eye but she couldn't concentrate. Memories of her grandfather kept coming back. Had he been murdered?

It was time to check on Alek again. No change. When she got back to the kitchen she turned on her laptop, went to the Der Spiegel website. They had the most up to date news on what was going on in Germany.

When she'd spoken to Henry Mowlam, he'd assured her that the situation there was a health emergency that few people outside the immediate family or friends of those who'd died were likely to get infected. She'd told him that Sean was there. The news didn't seem to surprise him. Mowlam asked her to call him if Sean didn't arrive back when he was supposed to.

That part of their conversation should have reassured her. But still she'd checked a half dozen websites covering the situation in Germany. Every one of them had said that the only people who'd been infected so far were refugees. One site had speculated that it was an Ebola-like disease that had been brought in from Rwanda.

A few comments under that article suggested that relatives of those infected should be forcibly quarantined. One commenter had pointed out that anyone in contact with infected refugees should be considered a possible carrier of the infection, as it had killed dozens already in Germany.

She would ask Sean to go straight to the doctor when he got back, get blood tests done, have a full check-up. Perhaps they should disinfect every item of clothing he was wearing, and throw out that stupid backpack he was using. Can you get hazardous waste disposal service at home, she wondered, like they have in hospitals?

In twenty-four hours he'd be home. He was going to be safe. They didn't need any more problems. They needed him back.

He knew how difficult Alek could be, especially at night. His occasional wails, when he had a nightmare reminded her of the horror movies she'd loved as a student, which she could no longer watch.

She made a cup of Camomile tea to calm herself, sipped at it, stared out into the garden. She would go up again in a minute, check on Alek. Then she had to do some work.

A Chinese dissident had sent them over a gigabyte of documents, which he claimed were Communist party records of corruption allegations made against senior officers of the Party that had not been acted on. Not only had she limited time to verify that the documents were genuine, matching them with samples they had access to, both for their content and for their file structures, but she would also have to deal with emails from U.S. bloggers, who had got wind of the leak.

All of this had come at exactly the wrong moment. She needed to get it out of the way quickly. She looked out the window, as the screech of a car coming to a halt reached her. Visions of Eleni laughing, but now dead, made Isabel hold herself tight. She prayed that whatever Eleni had got herself caught up in would stay well away from Sean and that he wouldn't bring any bad news back with him.

She stood and walked to the window. A light had gone on in an upstairs room in the house that backed onto theirs. It went off again. She tightened her arms around herself. Why the hell couldn't Sean stay out of trouble? He attracted it like bloody meat attracts sharks.

Some witch had said to her when she'd married him, that there are people who collect trouble all their lives, they just can't help it. It's to do with the star sign they're born under. She didn't believe in astrology, but it was looking as if the witch was right.

She closed her eyes and said another prayer to the God she barely believed in.

Was that her phone ringing? It was. She walked fast to it, found it on the table by the front door.

Sean's number. He must be psychic. He was calling to reassure her.

She smiled, wide.

She picked up the call, listened. All she heard was one word, spoken softly, before the line was cut.

"Help!"

Captain J.P. MacAllister, U.S. 7th Army, 45th Division, 3rd Battalion – Nuremberg April 24, 1945.
Field Report 45/4/21/7A/4 Status: Top Secret/LEVEL 1

This report covers classified activities at Nuremberg, after the surrender of the city April 20, by a Colonel Wolf, at that period / in command of the German units defending the city / 11:00A.M..

ORDERS
I received a radio order to investigate the site below Nuremberg Castle. The objective – Burg 13/26.

REPORT
Along with two staff sergeants, assigned from the special investigations team, we entered a basement at the lower end of the street, to which we had been directed by O.C. Colonel Wolf. We used explosive charges to open a basement office door.
Inside were boxes of files lined up against each wall.
Items of special interest in the basement are detailed in the list attached. One item, which I was asked to notify General Patton of immediately should I find it, was not in the basement.
A metal box, containing letters, bearing various seals was found. The box is under 24hr guard. Please notify the undersigned directly if there are any further orders regarding these letters.

Laurence O'Bryan

CONCLUSION
All orders regarding handling of items as detailed previously
45/4/21/7A/2 have been followed.

//I wish it noted that one of the staff sergeants, a Sergeant
O'Connor, made a sign of the cross when he saw the seals
on the above mentioned letters.

:ENDS/

33

Sean said nothing as his wallet was searched. The man doing it was dressed in black. His pale blue eyes, visible through small holes in a ski mask, glanced up at Sean occasionally. His sidekick was pointing a dangerous looking mat-black pistol at Sean. It had the letters - *HK* - embossed in orange on its side. He spoke fast to his colleague as the other man examined Sean's wallet.

The first man grunted as he looked at the credit cards. Then he pushed the wallet back towards Sean and motioned him forward.

Cold steel pressed into his side. He moved. The man who'd searched the wallet inserted a key into the door in the church wall. It swung inwards. The guard went through. Sean followed, after another vicious poke from the gun in his back.

They were in a hurry.

A vein throbbed in his neck. Cold sweat slipped down his back. What were they planning to do with him? He glanced around, hoping that someone might be passing, that they might see him. His effort was met by a clip from the Heckler & Koch on the side of his head and another hard push forward. Sparks of orange and white flickered in his vision as pain sliced through his head and down his back.

He put a hand to his forehead.

"Bastard," he hissed.

"Mund halten," said the man behind him.

Sean went through the door.

The first man walked ahead along the stone-flagged basement corridor. He went down the spiral staircase Sean had seen from the window. Sean got a poke in the back and another comment in German as he hesitated at the top of the stairs. He followed down. The stone walls around them were damp in patches. In places, green slime slid under his fingers when he touched the wall.

He glanced back. Might he be able to pull the bastard down on top of them and send them all falling down the stairs together?

There was a grunt behind him. The man had stopped. He was pointing his gun at Sean.

He kept going down.

Why hadn't they searched him properly up above? Then it came to him. They had to get him away from being seen or heard by anyone outside the church. He slowed, felt for his phone in the zipped pocket on the outside of his leather jacket, pressed on it, while it was still in his pocket, then slipped it into his hand. He reached to the side with his other hand, held the wall, hoping to distract the man behind him. His phone was in front of his chest. He pressed at it with the same hand that held it.

He glanced down. Why wasn't it responding? Was he down too far to get a signal? He coughed, held the wall, bent forward as if he was ill. His other hand was pressing at his list of recent phone calls.

And then it was connecting. He didn't hold it to his ear.

Isabel's name appeared on the screen.

"Halt!" came a shout behind him.

The line connected.

"Help!" he said.

The back of his head exploded in pain. He reached for the wall.

A clatter echoed as the phone fell onto the stone stairs and bounced from step to step. He slumped. The pain was intense, as if a nail had been driven into his head. He groaned. His head was spinning. He was going to fall.

"Schnell," came a shout from the man below.

He stumbled down, clutching at the wall. The stone was cold. Had Isabel heard him? A rush of guilt poured through him, then a surge of hope. She'd call the police. They'd come looking for him.

But had she heard him?

At the bottom of the stairs, there was a circular area with stone block walls. Heavy wooden doors were to the left and straight ahead. Both were closed. His phone was on the floor, in pieces. The glass front was shattered. The guard who'd been in front of him stamped on it as Sean reached the last step. Plastic and glass scattered across the floor.

The man reached down and collected the larger pieces, slid them into his pocket.

He motioned for Sean to raise his hands. "Hande hoch."

Sean complied.

The sidekick patted him down, slowly, examined the change in his pocket, the room card from the hotel. Then the other man patted him down a second time, ran his hands tight against his skin. What were they looking for? Sean's head was thumping fast with pain. He pressed a hand to his forehead. It felt wet. He took his hand away. It was stained with blood.

A dull shuddering noise had started up, as if an electric motor had been turned on nearby. The guard who'd stamped on his phone knocked on a wooden door at the bottom of the stairs. A shout in German came from beyond the door.

The door opened. A long stone corridor could be seen beyond it. It was dimly lit. A smell of damp and something rotten came out of it. A similarly dressed guard was behind the door. He muttered something when he saw Sean.

The shuddering noise grew louder. It sounded as if a truck was running up ahead. Cold steel poked into his back again. He followed the first guard down the corridor. Near the end, the guard pushed open a door and they entered a square stone-roofed room. The stone was darker here, much of it stained black and green near the floor.

Small niches had been cut into the walls. A raised stone area at the far end looked like an altar. A Star of David in the stone floor had been attacked at one time with chisels or other implements. Most of it was missing and only a mark in the underlying stone showed where its outline had been.

Four men in black were standing around a hole in front of the altar area at the far end of the room. They were looking down at someone else who was in a hole in the floor, and whose head only could be seen, wearing a red helmet. The yellow upright of a drilling machine could also be seen in the hole. It was moving, banging up and down.

A shout went up as Sean arrived. The drilling stopped. A man without a ski mask, with slicked back hair, exchanged words in German with the guard who'd led Sean down.

Sean didn't get near the hole, or see what they were drilling for, but he did hear something strange before the drill started up again. The sound of running water. Then he was pushed towards a smaller door in the far corner. He went through it with the cold muzzle of the gun pressed into his back. Now they were in what looked like the basement area of a medieval house. There were dark wooden joists above their heads and each wall had faded whitewash on it, from when it had been painted a long time ago.

In one corner there was a wooden staircase. Under the stairs there was pile of what looked like dead rats. The smell in the room was a sickening combination of mustiness and fear.

He put a hand to his nose. The drilling had started up behind them. He was pushed hard towards the stairs and for a horrible second he thought the guard might push him into the mound of rats.

But he didn't. He pushed Sean up the stairs. As he went up he could see what was under the stairs. It wasn't dead rats.

It was something sicker. Dead animals with shiny skins. Possibly river snakes.

He shivered, looked away.

The noise of the drilling stopped as he neared the top. A shout echoed, as if the men in the other room behind them had found something. The cold muzzle pressed into him again, deep into his side. Now he was at the top of the stairs going through a door. They were in what appeared to be the basement of a butcher's shop. There were bright lights in the ceiling and steel tables and hooks hanging from a rail attached to a low roof. Rows of different sized knives hung on a rail attached to the wall.

Giant steel vessels stood together along the far wall.

He looked around. This would be a great place to finish someone off. After you got your victim here, you could chop him into small pieces, before disposing of the blood and bones and mixing the body parts into some grisly concoction.

Fear comes in many forms. For Sean it came in the tightening of his muscles from his knees to his stomach and down his arms and a sickening churning sensation.

A large blue container stood by one wall. The guard pointed at it.

Sean shook his head, slowly. He wasn't getting into that.

The guard pointed again. Sean's was breathing fast. A huge mincing machine gleamed, where the guard was pointing, its giant circular maw ready for its next batch of meat.

The guard raised his gun, pointed it straight at him.

"You will do what I say, Herr Ryan, understood."
Sean took a step towards the man, looked him in the eye.
"Fuck you."

34

Isabel pressed the phone tight to her ear. The same message kept repeating in a chirpy tone. "The number you are calling is not available. Please try again later."

"No!" She wanted to throw the phone across the room.

Instead, she fished inside her bag, resting it on one of the kitchen chairs, and pulled out Henry Mowlam's card from the bottom. Sweat prickled on her brow. She went to the front door. She had a strong urge to leave straight away, find a flight, look for Sean. Now. But she knew that was crazy.

She tapped in Henry's number. He wasn't going to be happy, getting a call at seven thirty on a Sunday night, but she didn't care.

She stood near the door, as she waited for the line to connect. What would she do if she couldn't get him? She walked up the stairs, distracted. What time was the next flight to Nuremberg? She stumbled on a toy.

"Mrs Ryan, what's up?" Henry's voice. Thank God, and it sounded as if he'd sensed something was wrong.

"It's Sean. He's in trouble. He's in Nuremberg. He just rang me. Two minutes ago. I'll kill him, I swear. Can you help him, please, Henry?" Half sobs choked in her voice. She breathed in, steadying herself.

"Mrs Ryan. Slow down. Tell me what happened. Just the facts, please."

She told him all about Sean's call, about her fear that something had happened to him.

She ended with, "I should go there, tonight. I have to."

"No, Mrs Ryan. You don't have to. We have people on the ground in Germany. They can liaise with the police there. We'll put in a request for his phone to be tracked. You've got your son to look after."

"That was a statement, Mr Mowlam, not a request." She bit her lip. She wasn't going to be treated like an idiot. "I can't do nothing, while you liaise. I've seen what happens to international phone tracking requests. They can take days. I'm not going to wait here."

Henry sighed. "Does he have a location tracking app on his phone, Mrs Ryan?"

"Yes."

"Then we'll find him. What's his number?"

She gave it to him, regretting as she did that she hadn't got around to connecting Sean's phone to hers, so she could track it.

"You might remember I was an experienced field operator in Istanbul for the British consulate. I know the way things work, Mr Mowlam."

Mowlam, sighed. The noise was deliberately loud; she was sure of that. "Mrs Ryan, I am not casting doubt on your ability. But it is years since you were involved in any active service, even if you have kept your skills up to date. And you don't speak German, do you? Leave this to us."

He said that so definitely she felt anger rising inside.

"Will you provide assistance, that's all I need to know? Will you tell me if they find out where his phone is?"

Mowlam sighed, even louder this time. "When are you going?"

"I'll be on the next flight from Heathrow. I'll know what time that is as soon as I get to a computer."

"Hold on." There was a pause. The sound of keyboard clicks came down the line. Henry's voice came back on. "There's a flight at seven-thirty in the morning direct to Nuremberg from Stansted. Can you make that?"

"There's nothing earlier? Nothing tonight?" The sweat on her face was turning cold. She wanted to do something now.

She heard the sound of keys clacking again. "You could fly to Berlin tonight, then get a train. You'd probably arrive half an hour earlier then flying in the morning, after being up all night. Is that what you want?"

"No." It was her turn to sigh.

"I advise you not to go at all, Mrs Ryan. Think of your son."

She put a hand to her forehead. She was pacing the upstairs corridor now, zombie-like. Her head was bowed. How could he ask her to choose between her husband and her son?

"I can't...I can't just stay here, Henry." Tears sprang through her eyelashes. She wiped them away, fast. "I won't."

Henry's tone softened. "I understand, Mrs Ryan, but you must think about Alek."

"I am thinking about him. I'll call you when I'm in Nuremberg." She closed the call.

Ten seconds later it rang. It was Henry.

"If you insist on going, then I insist on dropping something in to you this evening."

"What?"

His voice dropped. "Will you be there in an hour?"

"Yes."

She called her sister who lived thirty minutes away. Jenny agreed to take Alek for a few days. Jenny and Isabel had been distant after their mother had died, but since Alek had been born they'd become a lot closer.

She said she'd be back for Alek by Wednesday evening. She said a prayer that Sean would be with her. This couldn't be anything that serious, could it? A shiver ran down her back at the thought. No, he'd be all right. He had the best survival instincts of anyone she'd ever met. They'd get through this.

She had to stay positive. She tried to read a Sunday paper on her iPad, even for a minute to look at the headlines, but she couldn't. There was way too much turmoil in her head. She paced up and down the kitchen instead.

Her concern for Sean was getting deeper the more she thought about it. Was this anything to do with his work, that paper he'd delivered at the conference? Some of the neo-Nazis who'd come slithering out of the woodwork since the refugee crisis, had been threating politicians and academics.

There'd been physical attacks too. The anti-refugee riots had brought out the thug element in German society.

The door buzzer sounded. She was at the door in two seconds. They'd had a new security camera installed, and toughened glass, but still she felt vulnerable.

She looked at the screen on the wall. It showed the porch outside the door. It was dark on their side road at the back end of the King's Road in deepest Chelsea, but she could see enough from the porch light to make out Henry Mowlam, MI5's finest. He was carrying a brown envelope.

Relieved, she opened the door. He had a long blue coat on. It looked as if it had been purchased that afternoon from a department store that catered only for mid-level government employees. Unusually, he was tieless. He didn't smile as Isabel let him in.

"Are you still insisting on going to Germany?" were his first words.

"My sister's husband is collecting Alek shortly."

He glared at her.

"Shall I take your coat?"

"This won't take long. May I have your phone, Mrs Ryan."

"Why? I'm sure you can monitor every call and Facebook message without seeing it."

He held his hand out.

"Come with me." She led the way down the corridor to the kitchen. Alek had appeared from his room. He was sitting in front of the internet connected TV in the far corner of the kitchen now watching YouTube. He glanced around as they came in. She waved at him, smiled, hoping not to worry him, then sat at the large, old fashioned kitchen table, and passed Henry her phone.

"Don't break it, please."

"I won't." He put the brown envelope down on the table, took a pin from his lapel and pushed the SIMM card holder out of her phone. Then he placed her SIMM on the table and opened the envelope.

Inside was a slim smart phone with no brand on it. It could have been an Apple prototype or a Samsung or any other brand, there was no way of knowing.

"This is the phone you'll be taking to Nuremberg," he said, as he placed her SIMM inside it.

"What's this phone going to do that mine can't?"

"It sends your current location to us directly at all times, and, if you press the front screen hard and fast, it will emit a 150 decibel shriek for exactly ten seconds. That will have anyone within five metres covering their ears in pain. It's not likely you'll need it, and I won't test it here with your son around." He glanced over his shoulder at Alek, then turned back to her.

"But the most important thing is that we'll know where you are at all times."

"Have you requested tracking on Sean's phone?"

"Yes, but I've had no response yet."

"I knew it. It will be days before they get back to you."

"I requested priority on this, but they do have an emergency situation going on over there."

Isabel picked up the new phone, switched it on. It asked for a password. She put in her own. It worked. They know everything. The phone screen wasn't the same as hers, but it had a messages icon and a contacts icon and weather and the other usual icons you'd expect.

"It doesn't have Facebook, Mrs Ryan, but I don't expect you'll be announcing where you're going."

"No, I won't."

"If you come across anyone from the German security service in your travels Mrs Ryan, tell them you know me."

She thought for a moment. "Will you tell them I'm going to Nuremberg?"

His expression didn't change. "Yes, Mrs Ryan. We work in cooperation with the BfV in Germany. We're both on the same side, despite what the EU haters might prattle on about." Now he smiled, but just a little. "Do you still want to go?" He stared at her, willing her to change his mind, it seemed.

"Yes."

"You should be aware that the infection that has killed 44 people in Nuremberg and the rest of Bavaria, and has now spread to Berlin and Hamburg. The death toll is predicted to reach hundreds, Mrs Ryan, possibly thousands. It is likely that the recent anti-refugee riots will get worse too. Victim blaming is common, when there's a chance the victims might infect you. Are you prepared for this?"

"Is it true that everyone who has died so far is from one ethnic group?" She raised her eyebrows.

"So far, that's correct. But this is not unexpected. Infections often spread to family and friends first, then beyond. It's only a matter of time before the epidemic reaches others. We don't believe there is any infection that targets one ethnic group exclusively. We expect to see all nationalities among the final casualties."

Isabel shifted from one foot to the other. "Is that all?" She had things to do. She had to pack for Alek, and for herself.

Henry didn't pick up the hint, or he deliberately ignored it.

"How is everything at InfoFreed, Mrs Ryan?"

"Everything is good, Mr Mowlam." She looked him straight in the face. Was he going to use this as an opportunity to try to get some leverage over her?

"I'm sure it is. The data security measures you implemented for them are very good, I hear."

He was well informed on many counts.

"Just one thing. Like you do, we recommend InfoFreed doesn't move to Iceland. Security there will be a little more questionable than it is here."

"You must be reading my emails regularly, Mr Mowlam."

He shrugged. "What do you expect?"

"Nothing less. You are supposed to be guarding the free world."

"And you're still going for the seven thirty flight in the morning?"

"Yes, don't you know that already, or are your internet systems a little clunky still?"

He didn't react to her comment. "I was alerted when you bought a ticket forty minutes ago, Mrs Ryan. What I was asking you, is whether you are going to use it after all that I have told you."

"If your partner was at risk, what would you do?"

35

"If you make any problems, that is where you will end up, Herr Ryan." The guard pointed at the gleaming mincing machine. He laughed. It was the laugh of a sadist enjoying himself.

"What the hell do you want from me?" said Sean. He stepped back from the guard, looked around for a weapon. There was nothing obvious and the guard's gun was still pointing at him. He would have to wait for his chance.

"What were you doing up above?" The guard aimed the gun at Sean's heart. "Answer me. We can dispose of you, turn every part of you into animal feed. I don't think the hamburger shops will say no." He grinned. "Now, tell me what you are doing here." His eyes gleamed with pleasure. "Go on, have a look inside these boxes to see what they make here."

He waved Sean towards the blue containers. The other guard was observing things with a twisted look on his face.

Sean walked toward the box, lifted the lid. Pink liquid sloshed around. His stomach rebelled at the stink of meat.

He dropped the lid, turned back to the guard. "A friend told me there was something buried under this church. I decided to have a look. I was going to leave when you found me. That's why I'm here. That's all I can tell you."

The guard's expression didn't change. He pointed at a door in the wall. It was wooden and looked like the entrance to a store room. "Get in there."

"No," said Sean.

"Do it now." He came towards Sean, raised his weapon, pointed it at Sean's head.

Sean shrugged, went towards the door. As he put his hand on it he turned.

"Someone will come looking for me. You won't get away with this."

"In."

The man pushed him hard in the back, as he opened the door. Sean fell forward. The only light in the room came from a small three-inch square opening above the door, which appeared to be there to provide ventilation. There was a wooden table at the far end of the room, pushed up against a wall. The table was bare. It was the only furniture in the room, which was a little wider than the reach of his arms and perhaps double that deep, with the roof only a foot or so above his head.

The door banged shut behind him. The light dimmed. The room was a gray mist now, illuminated by bars of thin light coming from the hole above the door. He went to the table, pulled it to the door, stood on it, looked at the hole, and checked if it could be expanded. It was surrounded with dull old-looking metal. There would be no easy way out. He walked around the room, paced the four walls slowly. There was definitely no other exit except through the door.

He sat on the floor. An iron weight had descended on his shoulders. He had brought all this on himself. If he hadn't started poking his nose in to what was going on here, he would be back in his hotel. He groaned to himself, got up, stood near the door, listened. He could hear talking outside. Then a bang, as a door slammed closed.

The good news was that it appeared the room outside was used regularly. Whoever the owner of the butcher shop was, they would probably be back in the morning to use the equipment.

The downside was, whoever worked out there had to be in on what was going on. Either that, or those guards would do something with him before the owner turned up. That thought made him close his eyes, press his fist into his forehead. What was he going to do when they came back?

He gripped his arms around himself. A distant rumbling sounded like a motorway far beneath his feet.

36

Vanessa Sheer scrolled down the screen of her laptop. The executive meeting room at the Nufaben facility was clinical and bright, although it had no windows. The doctor would be coming back in about fifteen minutes, after he had made the preparations.

On her screen was a graph of the monies on deposit in the various European regional offices of BXH. As usual, at the end of the weekend, the subsidiary Spanish and Swiss offices balances had jumped from money transfers.

The transactions of identity-disguised drug barons were the chief source of the weekly jump, she knew, but every transaction complied with World Bank rules for money laundering.

A vibration from her phone broke her concentration. She slipped it from the pocket of her Chanel trousers, smiled. It was the call she'd been waiting for.

She put the phone to her ear, listened for a minute to the politician on the other end, as he ranted about the deteriorating situation in Nuremberg, and the fear which was spreading fast now that the German people knew what was loose in their country.

"The streets are almost empty!" His voice was no more than a squeak. She could imagine him combing his fingers frantically through the few hairs drawn across his almost bald dome.

"I have appealed to the speaker of the Bundestag for a recall of parliament." He stopped his rant, probably to draw breath.

"What will you do if your appeal is granted?" She was waiting for the right answer. If the man didn't give it, he would be reminded of what he'd already agreed.

"We will seek to pass the law we discussed, which our sub-committee has drafted."

"Good. What did you call it in the end?"

"The Law for the Protection of Genetic Groups. This is similar to what you suggested. But we will raise the budget for the temporary rehousing and quarantine measures beyond what you suggested. No one will argue with any of this now. They would be run out of office by a mob if they did."

"Very good," said Vanessa Sheer. "We are right to protect genetic minorities. The German people will be proud of you. When will you present this law to the EU parliament?"

"Tomorrow. We have enough votes with the Hungarians and Poles and a few smaller countries to push it through as a recommendation to the European Commission. A few others will want an opt-out, but the rest will fall in line. The craziness over the refugee situation has changed everything. Who will stand against us?"

"Just make sure it happens."

"We will provide free transport vouchers and the promise of a bonus to each immigrant's bank account when they arrive for rehousing. That was my own little touch."

"What about the refugees who don't arrive at a facility within the next forty-eight hours?"

"They will be fined, as we agreed. There will be escalating fines, arrest warrants, detentions. We are lucky these crises are coming together." He sounded happy.

She didn't bother telling him that luck had nothing to do with it.

"You have all German patriots behind you."

"Your other important work is moving ahead, Vanessa?" He sounded excited.

She thought for a few seconds before responding.

"I've had confirmation that we will find the last piece of evidence we have been looking for soon."

"Sehr gut!" came the reply.

The line went dead. She went back to examining her screen. The only noise now was a hum from the powerful air conditioning. She didn't pay it any attention. She had a lot to do before Xena arrived.

37

Isabel held the handrail on the S-Bahn underground train. With its blue plastic covered seats and pale wooden walls it reminded her of pictures she'd seen of the London Underground in the Seventies. The train lurched around a curve, then stopped. They'd reached Nuremberg Hauptbahnhof, the central station. She moved with the stream of people getting off, her breath coming fast, as thoughts of what might happen, now that she was here, swirled inside her.

She pushed her way past pensioners with woolly scarves, young people in jeans and trendy leather jackets. She was elbowed by a boy with black spiky-Mohican hair and a silver chain hanging from his ear. He stared at her, muttered something she didn't understand. She looked away. She didn't care what these people thought. She had to find Sean.

A slow gray escalator took her up to the main hall. She made her way out of the front entrance. The station was a massive Gothic pile looming behind her. A long line of pale-yellow Mercedes taxis waited nearby. She opened the door of the first one, got in, put her black back-pack beside her.

She gave the name of Sean's hotel. The driver moved off, slowly. Tramlines stretched away in all directions. A medieval city wall with a round fortress tower, topped with a spiked roof and red tiles, sat directly opposite the station. Almost everything else was gray. There were twenty shades of it. A rush of traveller anxiety gripped her. She checked her pockets, her bag. She had everything.

They were weaving through narrow streets. After a few minutes the taxi dropped her outside the hotel.

"Please call Sean Ryan's room," she said to the receptionist.

There was a chance he was back, that his phone had been damaged or something had happened to it. Perhaps this was all a misunderstanding. It was the final slim hope she'd been clinging to during most of that morning's journey.

The receptionist grunted something she didn't understand. He was a large man with a disinterested expression. He checked his computer system, picked up a phone, dialled a number. "Herr Ryan is not available," he said, after listening for half a minute. He peered at his screen.

"Did he leave a note, any message? I am his wife." A black pit was opening up inside her.

He looked in a pigeon hole behind his desk then checked a large green leather diary. "I am sorry, we have no note or message from Herr Ryan." He looked at her, his face softening, sympathetic now, as if he was used to seeing wives looking for their husbands.

"Perhaps he will call you."

She shook her head, turned away, headed for the door. She had no choice now. She took her phone out, scrolled through a web page she'd saved, called the university where the conference Sean had been speaking at was being held. After ringing for a long time someone answered, and after explaining herself slowly, she was put through to a friendly English-speaking voice.

"How can I help?"

"I'm trying to contact Sean Ryan. He was speaking at your conference at the weekend. I was hoping he might still be there. I'm his wife." It was another long shot. The edge of the phone was tight against her ear.

"I am sorry. We didn't see Herr Ryan at all at our conference. We were expecting him but he did not arrive. I cannot help you." A note of pity had entered the woman's tone.

Isabel thanked her.

"Central Polizei, Jakobstlatz, bitte," she said to the driver of a taxi she found at the corner of the street.

He turned to her, said something fast in German. She shrugged in response. He waved a hand in the air, as if whatever he'd said didn't matter. Ten minutes later he pulled up at a modern office block with four storeys and a steeply sloping red tiled roof. The building looked as if it took up the whole of the block. A small blue sign jutting out from one corner had the word POLIZEI on it.

She paid the driver. He gave her an odd look. She ignored him, went into the station. The reception area was small, only ten foot wide. Blue plastic chairs were bolted into the floor along one side. A glass wall looked into an office where two policemen sat at desks.

A man with a straggly gray beard was talking in German, through a microphone set in the glass wall, to one of the policemen, seated on the other side. The man's voice was monotonous. He seemed to be reciting something. The policeman was tapping at a computer keyboard. Both officers wore light brown shirts. The officer visible on the other side of the room had dark brown trousers on, with a wide black belt, and a large black leather holster, with the butt of a gun glinting in it.

She didn't want to wait. She stood near gray beard. He glanced at her, opened his eyes wide, daring her to interrupt him. She took a step back, forced herself to breathe, to wait. She wouldn't get a helpful response if she pushed her way in front of someone.

The officer glanced at her, then continued his conversation with gray beard. It went on and on. Gray beard kept repeating something. The policeman's replies became longer, but he showed no impatience. After a while Isabel figured out he was repeating himself, but with extra details each time.

She could feel the light breakfast she'd had turning in her stomach, as flashes of what a life without Sean might be like ran through her mind. A numbness threatened to engulf her. Continuing on without him, was not a possibility she wanted to explore.

She was used to being loved, almost took it for granted. Losing him would be like losing a part of her body. The part that kept her alive.

Eventually, after Isabel sat down, holding her arms tight to herself for what seemed like hours, the old man turned and left and Isabel stood and approached the reception desk and the microphone.

"Do you speak English?"

"Yes, a little. How can I help?" The officer's smile was fleeting.

"I believe my husband is in danger. Can I report a missing person?" Her voice almost cracked as she spoke. Her words made what was happening real.

"How long has your husband been missing?" His tone was impersonal.

Isabel bit her lip. "Twenty-four hours." It was a lie. It was no more than twenty, but she wasn't going to be fobbed off.

"I'm sorry, unless we have evidence that," he paused, gave her a granite hard look, "a missing person's life is in danger, we are unable to conduct a missing person enquiry in the Federal Republic of Germany." He examined her face for her reaction.

"Didn't you hear me? My husband is in danger. He called me, yesterday, told me he needed help. His life is in danger. Please! He's not at his hotel!" The danger sounded less substantial now that she put it into words. She pulled her phone out of her jeans pocket, went to her call records, showed him the screen. A sinking feeling came over her.

What she was showing him wasn't evidence of a serious threat to Sean's life.

The policeman glanced at the call record, then back at her.

"What type of danger do you think your husband is in?" He glanced over her shoulder.

Someone had come in. There was a muttering and a shuffling behind her.

"I think he's been kidnapped."

"Has someone contacted you to tell you this?" There was weariness in his voice.

"No." She shook her head. "But he came to Nuremberg for a conference and never attended."

"Do you know any reason why he might be kidnapped?"

She stared at him, as she tried to work out her answer. "No, but I'm afraid he might have got caught up in something." As an explanation, it lacked substance. But what else could she say? She licked her lips. They were paper dry, thick. She wanted the questioning to be over, for them to do something, for them to help her.

The officer glanced behind her again, then spoke. "Please, what is your husband's full name?" He tapped at his computer screen, got her to spell Sean's name, their home address, her own name, gave the date he'd arrived, what he was doing in Nuremberg, and the name of the hotel he'd been staying in, and where she was staying.

"Wait over there," he said. She sat on one of the seats.

She checked her phone for messages, looked through her emails. Time slowed. She wanted to be doing something more. A woman, dressed in layers of ill-fitting clothes came in, was seen. Then a young man came in. Then he was gone and the little waiting area was empty again, except for her. She went back to the glass window. She couldn't just sit there, indefinitely.

"Please, what's happening?"

"Someone will come to see you, soon," was the reply.

She waited some more. Eventually, her stomach twisting, memories of Sean, and visions of an empty future swirling in her mind, she closed her eyes.

"Frau Ryan?" a plainclothes officer was holding the glass door to the right open. He held out his hand to her. "I am Kurt Dienelt. I am sorry for keeping you waiting. I am an investigating officer." He led the way down a corridor, up some shiny stairs and into a modern office with two desks and a window overlooking a dark inner courtyard.

"Please, sit." He pointed at a chair that faced the side of the desks. He sat at one of the desks. A stack of red plastic files rested in one corner of the desk. A thin computer screen stood at the other. A closed leather diary, pens, and a German flag on a tiny podium, sat in the middle.

"I met your husband yesterday, Frau Ryan. He seemed good then. What do you think has happened to him?"

She gulped. He'd seen Sean!

38

The tour guide smiled. It wasn't often he got so many question. The Frauenkirche was open to the public. The Nuremberg Meistersingers had just given a lunchtime recital, but he didn't mind showing this nun around. She had been sent specially by the senior administrator of the Diocesan Museum of Bamberg, a priest he knew well.

He touched the nun on her arm. She was taller than him, and he wondered where she might be staying. Perhaps she would go for a coffee with him afterwards? It wasn't often they got visitors from Rome.

"May I see the crypts?" said Xena. She pulled the wimple tight down over her forehead and looked at the tour guide's shoes. They were brown, highly polished. He clicked his heels together.

"But of course, Sister. We don't allow the public tours to visit all of the crypts, but in your case, I am sure no one will mind if I give you the full tour."

The sound of the last concert-goers exiting the front of the Frauenkirche echoed from the roof of the church and the high stone arches on both sides. The door he led her through had stone images of saints running up each side and a pointed three tier arch with small stone faces above. He turned on a single yellow light bulb above their heads before closing the door behind him.

"We don't want the public coming down here and getting lost, do we Sister?" He smiled at her. His small white teeth gleamed against his pale lips.

"Do people get lost down here, Father?" she replied, meekly. She gave him a small smile, then wiped it from her face and looked down at his shoes again.

"You could, Sister." He leaned towards her. "And please, do not call me Father. I am not ordained, yet. I am still a young man." He put a hand on her arm. "Follow me."

They passed a stone statue of a grieving Virgin Mary with the body of Jesus across her knees. There were blackened, half-finished, and unlit candles in a row at her feet. They reached a stone stairs leading downwards.

"These crypts used to be part of a synagogue that was on this site."

"There was a synagogue here?" she sounded genuinely interested.

"Yes, in the pogrom against Jews in 1349 about 500 were burnt to death on this site. Afterwards Charles IV gave the area to the Church. It's said the Church helped him raise the rabble that did the burning, but we don't believe that, do we?" He turned to smile at her as he reached the first stone landing. "In any case there are no records of sermons from that time."

"No, of course not. But it helped the church, did it not?"

He stopped at the next landing. The light was even yellower now.

"Your bag seems heavy, Sister." He pointed at the square black leather bag she held in her left hand.

"Prayer books. I have few possessions." She caught up with him, looked him full in the face. "Do you know of any small bed I might sleep in tonight?"

His face flushed. He blinked and swallowed.

"I'm sure we can find a place for you to lay your head, Sister." He continued on down. At the bottom there was a modern wooden door. He opened it with a key, reached inside the door and turned on a row of frosted glass lights set into the walls.

"The crypts, Sister. They extend to a point directly under the altar. It is said that masses were held down here when the city was threatened. I believe members of our hierarchy stayed here when the Americans bombarded the city in 1945." He pointed at a row of wooden tables.

She strode up the centre of the wide, stone-floored open space. "This is wonderful. What's going on under the altar Father?"

"Aaah," he said. "They are building a wooden staircase to a trapdoor in the apse. There is a plan to open this whole floor up to visitors one day."

Xena put her case down. "Show me."

39

"Sean called me last night," said Isabel. "He asked for help. Can you find him, please?"

Kurt rubbed a hand across his forehead. "We will do everything we can." He looked sympathetic. "Is there anything you can tell me, that might help us?"

She shook her head. Then she remembered about the paper he was planning to give at the conference. He'd told her about locals denying that there were any undiscovered mass graves around Dachau concentration camp, near Munich.

"Is it possible someone objected to the paper he was going to read at the conference?"

Kurt looked at her. "After I received the note that your husband was missing, a few minutes ago, I spoke with the conference staff, where you reported he was speaking. They said there were no threats or any incidents at any conference event."

"But there were objections to the paper he was going to deliver." She said it forcefully. She wasn't going to be fobbed off.

"Yes, but there is no record of any threats. Perhaps I might ask you about your relationship with your husband. How is that?"

She stared at him, her hands tightening into fists at the unspoken implications. "Our relationship is good. We have a good marriage. No problems. No problems whatsoever." She forced those last words out one by one.

There was a noise behind her. She turned. A middle-aged man with curly black hair and a large face had come in. He nodded at Kurt, then left the room.

"That was my partner. Would you like some coffee, Frau Ryan, or tea?"

"Coffee, please." She could manage a coffee, if it meant she could keep going.

After Kurt returned, a minute later – he must have gotten the coffee from a machine nearby – she said, "You don't think this has anything to do with Eleni Kibre's murder, do you?"

Her hand trembled as she raised the thin plastic cup to her lip. After sipping at it, she held the cup away from her, as if afraid it might fall from her fingers. The coffee was weak, hot.

"We do not know that," said Kurt.

Isabel stared at him. "Could the same person who murdered Eleni, have taken my husband?" She had to put the cup down. Her arm felt weak. It was hard to take in everything that was happening. She felt as if she was watching someone else go through it all, that she was just observing everything.

"Such a thing is possible, but let's wait to see what evidence our investigation uncovers, before we come to any conclusion, ja?"

The other policeman returned. He started speaking rapidly in German to Kurt. Sean's name was mentioned twice. Isabel could do no more than interpret their expressions. Kurt looked pensive, almost angry. Finally, he ended the conversation with a stroke of his hand and a few loud words in German. "Scheisse," was one of them.

He turned to her. "There was a request last night from our London colleagues at the Metropolitan Police. It was about your husband. Unfortunately, most of our available officers are engaged on a large investigation at present, so there may be a delay in dealing with their request." He paused.

Isabel picked up her coffee, sipped it. Henry Mowlam must have asked the Met to start a search for Sean. There could be no other reason for them contacting the police here.

"I am sorry, we have had over fifty unexpected deaths in Nuremberg in the past twenty-four hours," said Kurt. He turned to her. His eyes were red-rimmed. "We are overstretched already, visiting each family in our area to . . ." He stopped, abruptly.

The other officer had interrupted him. He was speaking rapidly in German. When he finished he stood, left the room.

Kurt stood. "I will call you when our investigation is finished," he said. "I have been summoned to a meeting. I am sorry. I will make sure that your husband's hotel security system recording is viewed, and also the one at the university in case he went there. I will call you if I have any news." He frowned. "Do you know if he had any other friends in Germany?"

Isabel stayed seated. She needed to impress on this policeman that Sean's disappearance was a serious matter. It wasn't a case of a philandering husband running off with some younger woman he'd met, and his distraught wife trying to track him down.

"No, I don't know any others."

Then, as if an afterthought had struck him, he asked, "Was there any interest in the paper your husband was presenting, back in England?"

"Yes, there was." Her voice had a shake in it. She clenched her jaw. "Someone approached me about it only the other day."

"Can you tell me the name of this person?"

Kurt was standing over her.

"I'd rather not say right now. It was an old man. I don't want to drag him into this."

Kurt looked unmoved, as if he'd heard enough sob stories to turn any heart to marble.

"What was this man's interest in Herr Ryan's paper?"

"He spoke about uncovering secrets from the Nazi era."

"Why was he interested in all that?"

She hesitated, then blurted it out. If it helped Sean, it had to be done. "He claimed he had letters from that time."

"We get a lot of this, Frau Ryan. Most of these Nazi truthers, as we call them, have fanciful ideas, but no evidence that any of their claims is true. Did you see these letters?"

"I saw photographs of them."

Kurt smiled. "May I have the name of this person, and their contact details?"

"I don't have that with me."

Kurt took his jacket from the back of the chair. "Please, send me the details, Frau Ryan." He put his jacket on. "We are interested in any new evidence about Nazi crimes."

Isabel stood.

"Your husband's work is important. Thank you for coming here." He motioned to the door.

Isabel went first, then followed him down the corridor. She was wondering what she was going to do next; go back to Sean's hotel, walk the city looking for him? Neither option was appealing. There had to be something else she could do. She couldn't just fly back to London.

"Have you found out who murdered Eleni Kibre?" She asked as they went down the stairs.

"Not yet."

On their way out he took her mobile phone number and promised to call her if he had any news. She reached out and took his arm. She gripped it tight. "Did he tell you he was going anywhere else in Nuremberg?"

Kurt put a hand on her shoulder. "Frau Ryan, we are doing everything we can to find your husband. Wait for my call. I will call you."

She tightened her grip on him.

"Where can I go while I wait? I have to do something?"

He breathed in hard. "Go to the Frauenkirche, if you wish. I believe Sean went there. Jerome claimed he was interested in an archaeological dig that's going on there, but I went there already. There is no dig. There was no Sean. He was mistaken. But if you want something to do, have a look around there."

She found a taxi, took it back to Sean's hotel. There were no rooms available, but they pointed across the street to another hotel, the Berliner, where she got a room. The hotel was in the same class as Sean's, clean, modern, with a small, bright reception area. She had a quick shower, then went out. She couldn't stay in the room. It felt like a prison cell. The condemned cell. And she was waiting for the worst news imaginable.

The receptionist, an ancient hippy, smiled at her as she passed. She'd loaded a map of Nuremberg and an app guide to the city onto her phone. She stopped at a cafe on the corner nearby, ordered a coffee and the lightest food she could find, a small round bagel with a thin slice of white cheese on it, to keep up her strength. She took a few bites, while she looked at the map and guide on her phone. Then she couldn't eat any more. The two bites of bagel felt like a slippery stone in her stomach. She sipped her coffee.

The onscreen map wasn't much good, the images were too small, but the guide did list the major churches in the city. She looked at the time. It was almost three o'clock. She worked out where the Frauenkirche was in relation to the café, read how it was described online.

Apparently, it was the symbol of Nuremberg. The market square in front of it was the place where Adolf Hitler had been filmed receiving salutes from thousands of robot-like

Nazi followers in *Triumph of the Will*, the most famous Nazi propaganda film of the 1930's, when he was increasing his grip on Germany.

She left the restaurant, walking fast. The streets were bustling with shoppers. She passed a corner with a bread shop with giant rounds of black bread in the window and there it was: the Frauenkirche. It loomed like a giant black wedding cake against the gray clouds that filled the sky. There was building work going on at one side. Men were erecting scaffolding. Had the policeman been wrong?

She walked quickly towards the church, passing wooden stalls selling cheese and olives and wooden toys and organic drinks, all set up in the cobblestoned square.

As she reached the metal barrier around the church her heart was pounding. Maybe she'd find out what had happened to Sean or at least find some trace of him that the police had missed.

This was exactly the sort of place he would have been interested in. Perhaps something had happened to him when he came here. Perhaps he'd fallen, injured himself, knocked himself out. He could have been taken to hospital, concussed.

She looked through the mesh of the metal barrier. There was no obvious hole for Sean to fall into. The scaffolding wasn't surrounding a dig. They were doing something above ground. It felt as if a hand was squeezing her heart. She hugged her arms around herself.

A building worker was having a cigarette beside a side door of the church. She waved at him. He was half facing her, so she wasn't sure he could see her. He didn't respond. He began talking to another man, who approached him. He also had a yellow hat on.

Isabel raised her voice, rattled the wire mesh.

"Bitte! Bitte!" Please, was one of the few words she knew in German.

The first man looked at her. He said something to his colleague then he came over to her, smiling.

"Yes? Can I help you?" he said in English. His accent was strong, as if he had gravel in his mouth.

"Is it that obvious I'm not German?"

"Yes."

"I'm looking for my husband. He went missing somewhere around here yesterday. I was wondering if anyone was injured here yesterday or taken to hospital."

He shook his head. "I can't help you," he said. "We only started here this morning. We are fixing new lights to the church." He pointed above his head.

She looked up. There was a row of grime-covered lights at the edge of the roof.

Then he pointed across the square. A fire engine with its blue light spinning was coming towards them. Its siren grew louder by the second. Isabel felt dizzy. Was this something to do with Sean?

40

Xena turned and looked back. Already she could hear the wail of emergency vehicles. She smiled. It would not be easy for any fire engine crew to stop what she'd started.

Few would understand the irony of a church built on the burnt-out ruins of a synagogue being burnt in its turn, but it was enough that it should happen. The wheel had turned.

Now it was time to do what she'd come here to do while the city was busy with its fate.

41

Isabel waited as the fire crew approached. She looked up at the tiered front of the church. She saw why they had come. Flames at the rear created a red glow behind the high frontage. A blue clock stood out half-way up the central spire. The blue stood out against the glow. A second fire tender had arrived, then a police van, it's blue light flashing rapidly, it's siren blaring, mingling with the others.

Two policemen set up blue plastic barriers at the far end of the square in front of the church. Another one began moving people back behind them. The man Isabel had been talking to had disappeared when she turned back to say something to him. She stepped back,

Was Sean in there? Anxiety pulled at her, then a sickening guilt. She should have told him this was not a good time to present his paper in Germany. Maybe if she had, he wouldn't have come here.

As the policeman approached her she looked around for somewhere else to watch what was happing. There was a pancake shop at the corner of the square.

She'd have a good view of the church from there. The area in front of the Frauenkirche was completely blocked off now. She made her way around to the café. It was modern, welcoming looking.

She ordered a coffee, sat at a table outside facing the church. An ambulance had arrived but its doors were still closed. That had to mean there were no injuries, yet. Didn't it? Something tightened inside her as she waited. Around her people were gesturing towards the Frauenkirche, talking to each other.

She thought about Alek back in England, how he'd hugged her when he was leaving, how sweet and vulnerable he'd seemed. How would she tell him, if something had happened to Sean? The tightness moved to her chest. She took out her phone, texted her sister. She kept her breathing slow and steady as she waited for a reply. It came in less than a minute.

All good here. Did you find him?

Not yet, she replied.

She sighed. A man at the table next to her gave her a benevolent smile.

Minutes passed. Another fire truck arrived. But no more ambulances. Firemen came out of the church, went to the ambulance, had a conversation with its driver, who stepped out to talk to them. Then they went back inside. The ambulance moved, parked further away. Two ambulance crew men got out, walked around, began smoking.

Isabel opened the guide to Nuremberg on her phone again. Should she wait here some more? She stared out the window. The crowd looking towards the church was bigger now. Hoses snaked into the front of the building. Black smoke billowed behind where the other fire tender was now parked. The red glow could still be seen, flickering. There was a sulphurous, unpleasant smell in the air too. It made her nose twitch.

She put her head in her hands, closed her eyes. Kurt had been right. There was no dig at the Frauenkirche. What the hell would Sean have done if he'd come here and discovered that? She looked at her phone, opened the app guide to Nuremberg.

Maybe she could visit the other big churches in the city centre. That's exactly what he would have done. The main ones looked to be in walking distance. After that she could head to the nearest hospital. She had to be sure she had done everything she could, just in case he had ended up in one of them.

Please, she prayed, don't let anything bad have happened to him. She stared at the church, watching a fireman coming out and heading to the tender. Maybe she should wait a bit more. The tightness in her chest was back.

Should she go or wait? She wrapped her arms tight around herself, rocked back and forward. Her hands were fists. She had to think about something else, not about Sean being dead. Waiting for him here was just making her feel worse. Every muscle in her body ached, as if some slow-acting poison had been given to her. She looked at her phone again, held it up, stared at the images of the other churches in Nuremberg, not taking in half of the words beside each of them.

She shook her head, trying to dispel the tightness inside. She had to be strong for Alek, for Sean. She made a decision. She would search all the obvious places in the city he might have gone to. She wouldn't give up while there was anywhere else to look.

She stood. Her next stop would be St. Lorenz's. Then she would visit St Sebald's. There was also another smaller church to visit.

Ten minutes later, after a brisk walk, she was inside the giant dark Gothic wonder of St Lorenz's. This was more of a tall, traditional style church than the Frauenkirche. She went inside with a gaggle of tourists through a high side door. There was conservation work going on in one of the aisles. She walked slowly around the inside of the building, taking in the high, dark, interior.

A group of priests were talking animatedly to three men in hard hats and orange overalls. They were eyeing the tourists, as if wondering whether they should close the church. An area at the front, around the apse, was cordoned off with shiny red and white plastic barriers. This could be an archaeological dig. She stopped at the barrier, waiting to see if any of the workers or priests would come to the edge of the cordoned off area, so she could talk to them.

But none of them did. She waited some more, then moved one of the barriers and went towards a priest who was arranging prayer books at the edge of the altar.

"Excuse me, Father, is there an archaeological dig going on here?"

The priest turned to her. His English was halting but clear.

"No, no, you must not come here. We are preparing for renovation work on our altar. Please, you must go. It is forbidden for you to be here."

She went outside, headed for St Sebald's.

She stopped at a pharmacy, an Apotheke, on the way, got something for her headache, swallowed it with some water they gave her. There was a bookshop beside it. Perhaps a better guide to the city might help. People were pointing at the skyline. She turned and saw an orange glow in the direction of the Frauenkirche.

The bookshop was almost empty. There was an old man in a far corner and a tall young man at the cash point. She found some guidebooks in English, picked one that would fit in her jacket pocket. As she was paying, she looked at some notices on the front of the cash desk. There was a Wagner concert coming up in St Catherine's.

She paid, went outside, stopped at a café nearby, sat on a chair outside without ordering anything. She read through the section on St Catherine's in the guide. It was a church that hadn't been repaired after it had been damaged in the last days of the Second World War. It was used as an open air concert venue now. It had originally been a Dominican convent, founded in the thirteenth century. The church had been the inspiration for an opera by Wagner, The Meistersingers of Nuremberg.

As a waiter came out she shook her head, then headed back to the bookshop to check when the concert was taking place. She went straight to the poster. The concert wasn't on for another ten days, but there was a cancelled sticker at the top of the poster, which she hadn't noticed before.

"Why is this concert cancelled?" she asked the woman behind the counter, who was smiling at her.

"Archaeological work," she said. "They are doing it for the last week there." Isabel was already gone. She wasn't running, but she was moving fast enough to attract the attention of passers-by. Hearing someone running behind her, she turned. All she was saw a mass of people who seemed to be all heading towards the Frauenkirche.

She looked up. The red glow was filling the darkening sky.

42

Sean banged the door again. His mouth was dry. He'd hit the door several times. The only response had been echoes. This time was no different.

He sat back, rocked from side to side. He wasn't going to scream. They wouldn't get that pleasure.

Whoever was keeping him here was taking their time about deciding what to do with him. That was good news, at least. It meant either they hadn't finished with him, or they had to wait for someone else to decide what to do.

Maybe they'd just leave, send a message to the authorities about where he could be found. That would be good.

But he knew that was wishful thinking. They could also be waiting for an opportune moment to kill him. Perhaps they had someone for that job, who would be arriving soon.

He stood, walked to the back wall, then to the door again, as he'd done hundreds of times since he'd been locked in.

It takes a certain type of individual, he knew, to be able to kill someone. He'd taken a life once, but that had been in self-defence. He'd never murdered just to silence someone. What makes a person capable of doing that?

Whatever these people were working on in that other room was probably just taking longer than they'd expected.

But what the hell were they doing digging down here? And was any of this a connection to Eleni's murder? There were too many questions to which he had no answers.

He thought about Isabel. She might come to Nuremberg if she'd heard his plea for help. He wasn't sure if that was good news or bad. It could easily be both. At least there was a sliver of hope. But every time he thought about it, a well of fear accompanied it.

The last thing he wanted was for these bastards to do anything to Isabel.

He stopped, sat down with his back to the cold, rough stone wall. If anything happened to her or to Alek, he could never forgive himself. He should have just gone back to London. He listened. Was that someone coming?

There was definitely a grinding noise. He'd heard it a few hours before. Now it had started up again. It was louder, if anything, this time. And it was definitely coming from somewhere below him. He put a hand on the stone floor. Yes, it was vibrating just a little, but it was unmistakable.

He stood, tried to get a sense of how deep below him the noise was coming from. It couldn't be that far if he was feeling it, could it? Then the noise changed. It was louder, more high pitched than before. He counted seconds. One thousand. Two thousand. Three thousand. Then it stopped, but only after an echoing rumble spread through the floor of the little room like a wave.

He put his ear to the ground, fancied for a moment that he could hear voices, but there was almost nothing to be heard now, just an echo in his mind of the rumble that had gone before. But something had definitely happened. The grinding noise didn't restart. And now the silence was ominous.

If they were waiting to make some breakthrough before dealing with him, what he'd heard could be that breakthrough. The silence grew by the second, like an oppressive force bearing down on him.

Then he heard a different noise.

The sound of footsteps echoing from the room outside. The door opened. Light flooded in, blinding him.

"Come," said a voice.

43

Isabel entered the grounds of the church through a gateway in the wall that connected the cobblestoned area in front of it to the street. She walked to the metal gate which filled what had been the main doorway of the church. It allowed visitors to see inside. The gate was locked.

Along one side of the church there were metal barriers at head height, running about six feet away from the wall of the church all the way to the back, enclosing it. You couldn't see through them. They had orange plastic sheeting on the far side, but after walking along them she found a small gap in the plastic to peer through. There were no signs of a dig on the other side. It looked as if the barrier was simply protecting the wall, which loomed above her, reaching about twenty feet into the air.

This side wall of the church was made of the same black-streaked stone as the other churches she'd been to in Nuremberg. Towards the back of the church there was a series of high pointed-arch stone windows with thick opaque glass where the stained glass must once have been.

It was quiet at the far end of the church. There was a building, it looked like the back of a school, to the right, and ahead there was what looked like an office building that had once been someone's house. Both had windows with lights on at the first floor, but she could see no one near the windows and the fifty-foot-wide cobbled space between the church and the offices had a deserted feel, as if few people ever came here.

She walked slowly. She could see the top, the arch of a doorway. Her foot hit something. She looked down. There was a black rubber encased flashlight on the ground. It was shiny, new looking. Someone had dropped it recently.

She turned it with her shoe. There were no markings on it. It looked like something a security person would use. She pushed it towards the metal barrier with her foot. She walked on, noticed that one section of the barrier had a hole at ground level, where the wire mesh was pushed in. It looked as if someone had pushed a way through. Her heart pounded. Had Sean come this way?

She looked around, turning 360 degrees to see if she was being observed. There was no one nearby. She had to move quickly. A few people had passed a minute before, heading through the church grounds to an exit at the back. But there was no one around now. She bent down, as if tying her laces. She couldn't just walk away and wonder for the rest of her life if this was where he'd been. She took one last look around, then lowered herself to the ground and pushed her way under the mesh.

Grit stuck to her hands. The bottom edge of the wire barrier snagged at her. She moved her shoulders, came unstuck, pushed forward.

The only sign that something was going on behind the barrier were tools lying on the ground near a doorway set lower than the smooth cobbles around the church.

She heard a noise, a woman talking in German, perhaps on the phone to someone. She stepped to the side, waited, holding her breath, as the sound of the voice grew, then dimmed. When the woman was gone, she breathed deeply. Then she went to the pile of tools. There were two shiny steel shovels, a green wooden sweeping brush and a red plastic bag about three-foot-long, with words in German on it in small white letters.

She looked at the door. It was down a few steps to her left. If there were shovels that had to mean someone was digging here. And from what she'd seen they weren't doing it around the church. They had to be doing it inside, somewhere in the basement. There was still no sign of any guards. She went down the steps, put her hand against the ancient wood of the door. It was blackened with age and rough like bark under her fingers.

She leaned close to it and listened. She could hear nothing except the low hum of a car passing in the street. She felt for the metal door handle, turned it. It was cold. The door opened smoothly without a squeak. She could feel her heart beating in her throat. She had a sudden sense of regret, that she had allowed things to come this far, trespassing. Should she go back?

No, she couldn't.

She listened at the doorstep, ready to close the door and flee the way she had come if she heard someone. She heard nothing.

She looked back over her shoulder. There were no sounds except the distant rumble of cars.

She waited, listening, a lightness filling her stomach. The place was deserted, but possibly not for long with those tools outside. She had to move. She took a few steps onto the stone corridor that stretched away to the left and right. There was an opening just ahead to the left in the inside wall. To the right the stone-lined passage curved away around the back of the church. She walked to the left, toward the opening in the wall. It led into a circular stone stairs leading down.

She stood at the top, peering into the well of the stairway. A smell of dust and loose earth filled her nostrils.

Voices!

There were people here. They were far off, so she didn't move. All she did was stand and listen, trying to work out where the echoing voices were coming from. She strained forward to see if she could understand anything they were saying. But they didn't seem to be coming from below. The urge to find Sean, was getting stronger. She balanced on her toes, turning, a hand holding the edge of the wall, ready to move if the voices came closer.

She was really hoping to hear Sean's voice. It was unlikely, but that was what she wanted. No matter what happened, she wanted to hear his voice again.

The voices were getting louder. She considered her options. It had been fortunate that there weren't security guards about when she'd entered. Perhaps they'd just gone further along the corridor for a few minutes, and they were coming back. Were they about to find her, trespassing? She stood, transfixed to the spot. Her instincts were telling her to hide or to run, but where could she go?

Could she say she was exploring if they caught her? She headed down the stairs.

At least they wouldn't see her down here.

She went down, fast, quietly. The stairs became a spiral. Within seconds she was in gloom, lit only by occasional dim yellow bulbs. The voices were growing quieter, as if whoever was up there was standing talking. She thought she recognised one of the voices, the second voice, but she dismissed the thought. Why would she recognise someone speaking German?

She kept going down, but slower now. The stairs had to lead somewhere. Had the Dominicans constructed crypts during one of the wars that had passed through the city? The guilds had rebelled against the patricians several times, she'd read. In 1420 A.D. parts of the city had been destroyed. She tried hard to keep the noise of her footsteps to a minimum as she continued on down, but her foot hit a stone sending it tumbling down the stairs.

She stopped, listened.

There was nothing to hear now, except her own shallow breathing and the thumping in her chest. She went down another turn, her hand brushing the wall to guide her. Was there a way out? Had she discovered where Sean had gone? Perhaps he was trapped somewhere down here.

Then the lights went out.

She had an urge to stop, to go back, as the darkness thickened around her, but she knew she couldn't. She had to keep going. She had to see what was down here.

The gloom was total now. Her heart racing, she took out her phone and switched it on. The sight that greeted her made her wince.

Curtains of cobwebs hung above her head. Some extended up the stairs behind her. A slight wetness she felt on the walls now was a thin green mould. It glistened.

A spider on the floor, a black giant, half as big as her hand, scuttled away from the light. She stood still, urging her breath to calm. Should she go back up? Maybe the men had gone. Maybe she was just being stupid continuing on down. Then a distant noise echoed down to her, followed by a shout.

She kept going down, but faster now, keeping her phone on. The slime was thicker the further down she went, and the cobwebs denser with each turn of the stairs. Finally, she reached the bottom. It looked like the bottom of a well. There was water on the floor, piles of green slime by the walls and a single door straight in front of her. The door was open. She shone her phone into the passage beyond, stepped through tentatively. Water sloshed against her shoes.

She moved forward. The passage was head height, cobblestone walled, and it had a curved cobbled ceiling. There was a pungent damp smell and the air was warm and thick.

There was also a noise in the distance, a soft rumbling, as if there was a machine somewhere down here. This was exactly the sort of place Sean would end up. She took one last look back up the stairs. A voice in her head said *wait, maybe these people will help you,* but she ignored it. She had to see where the passage led.

44

"You're late," said Vanessa Sheer. She closed the screen on her laptop.

"The fire was slow to start," said Xena. She glanced around the meeting room. There was no one else in it and no obvious security camera.

Vanessa waved at a steel and leather chair on the opposite side of the table.

Xena stood behind the chair, reached with a hand and pushed the chair a little to the side. She crossed her arms.

Vanessa had her phone in her hand. She typed the word *kommen* into a message and pressed *senden*.

"You seem anxious, Xena. Is there a problem?"

"You are the one with the problem."

Vanessa raised an eyebrow. "If this is about your work, it's your choice how you carry out our instructions. I don't ask you to make people suffer." Her eyes stayed on Xena's.

Xena leaned across the table. "I will do each job the way I decide. You knew what you were getting when you took me on. I proved my worth for you in Manhattan and I almost got killed for you in Jerusalem." She leaned forward some more, until her face was half way across the table, her eyes wide and angry. "I was told the only people who would die would be those who deserved it. You deceived me."

"Who didn't deserve to die?" Vanessa leaned back. She knew the door behind would open in the next minute or so. There was nothing to fear.

"Eleni Kibre."

"She was going to expose what we do. She had to die."

"What was it she was going to expose?"

Vanessa stared at her. "We all want the same thing. You really must trust me. You really must do what I say."

The door behind Xena opened. Doctor Brandt walked in.

"Can I be of assistance?" he said, looking at Xena.

"Herr Doktor, please show this lady out. Our meeting is over." She turned to look at Xena.

"You will travel to Cairo. Go to our contact there as soon as you arrive. We have more work for you. Urgent work. And..." she paused. "Be assured that every job you do for us brings what you wish for forward." She turned to the doctor. "The shipment has been despatched?" The doctor nodded. She picked up her phone, began checking messages.

Xena was glaring at Vanessa. The doctor took a step towards her, put a hand out, as if to take Xena's arm.

Xena twisted away, strode to the door. She opened it gently. And on the way down the corridor, as they passed a ladies' toilet, she said, "Herr Doktor, I need your advice." She smiled, showing a row of perfect white teeth.

He didn't return the smile. "In what way?"

"It's personal. I would like your opinion on something." She pulled her black shirt up high with her left hand. As the doctor stared at the scar where her breast should have been, she slipped her knife from the back of her jeans, where she'd hidden it behind the metal and leather belt she wore, and took a step toward him. She moved fast, put the point of the blade up close to his eye.

"One stupid move and I'll bring light into your brains, good doctor. Go into that toilet, now." She nodded towards the nearby door.

She locked the door behind them. It was a single person toilet, like the one she had used near the reception area.

Five minutes later she exited the toilet and strode back up the corridor. When she reached the door to the meeting room, she paused. She moved the knife from one hand to the other, then back again. Both hands had blood on them. The knife slipped easily from her fingers as it went back and forth. She rubbed her forearm across her forehead, stopped moving the knife, put her hand forward.

When she tried the handle it wouldn't open. Two seconds later an alarm rang out in the corridor.

She looked around. There was an air ventilation grill high up on the far wall. It was small, but it would have to do. She ran to it, jumped up to catch the edge and slipped her knife between the unit and the wall until it was all the way in.

The cover popped. She jumped again, slid inside.

45

The light from Isabel's phone showed a long tunnel stretching away into darkness. Her eyes narrowed. Her skin prickled. This was not going to be easy. Memories of a tunnel she'd explored years before came back to her. She'd almost become trapped then. She didn't want to go through all that again. Her foot kicked something. She looked down.

It was the remnants of a canvas bag with a red cross on it. There were stains all over the bag. It looked like something from an old Second World War movie. Could it be real? Maybe General Patton's men had come down here after they took Nuremberg, in one of the last battles of the war, and one of its fiercest.

She kept going, walking rapidly, her head ducked to avoid knocking it on anything. After walking about twenty feet a turn to the right came into view. She stopped. The passage led on to a door, far off, deep in gloom. Would it open? She didn't want to get stuck in a dead end.

Another doorway loomed in the right hand wall. It was closed. She put her ear near it. She could hear voices. She looked on down the passage. The walls further along were made of thin red bricks, broken away in places, and there was rubble from the wall on the red, earth floor.

She held her phone forward, kept going down the corridor. She wanted to explore as much of this place as possible. She reached the door at the end, pushed at the ancient gray wood. The door didn't open.

She turned the handle, tried pushing again. It groaned slightly against the wet stone floor, then opened enough to slip through. She peered into the corridor beyond. It curved away into darkness.

She'd entered a labyrinth of underground tunnels. She'd read about the tunnels under Paris and Rome, and that other cities often had them, so it shouldn't have been unexpected that Nuremberg had similar tunnels, but still she felt uneasy.

The corridor sloped upwards here and was dry. It branched left and right. She took the right hand tunnel and came to an arch in the side wall. She peered into it, lighting the space with her phone.

The area beyond the arch was large, square, and had a low ceiling. Its walls were of a similar thin red brick to the passageway. In places there were holes in the walls and piles of bricks on the floor. Three doors stood in the wall at the far end of the room. She walked past each one, opened them, slowly. They led into smaller rooms, storerooms perhaps. When she went into one of the rooms she changed her mind.

They weren't store rooms. They were cells. And their doors, old and heavy, swung slowly. She checked the main room again. Rusty iron manacles hung from one wall, high up. Below them there were wooden beams, in a jumble, and what might have been ancient leg irons, and then she saw two giant rusty-iron face masks lying open behind the beams.

She peered down at them, moving her phone to look inside them. Three-inch-long spikes on the inside would cut into anyone's eyes who had the mask placed on their head. The mask also had slits near the spikes, so whoever was suffering could see who was torturing them, presumably. And whoever was doing the torturing could see the bloody result of their work.

Isabel shivered as she looked at the gaping masks. Who had been put into them? Poor bastards, whoever they were. And who had stood around and ordered it done, and watched as the masks were closed and the spikes tore deep into their faces?

She looked back at the door she'd come in through. Was anyone following her?

She stepped away from the masks. She'd remembered something else she'd read; that torture was used in Nuremberg until the nineteenth century, and that the town had exported torture implements all over Europe. She looked around the room.

The only thing out of place were two bags on a dry spot in one corner. They looked like bags of cement.

She turned off her phone. There were voices in the corridor speaking German. One of the voices was a woman's. And there was a light approaching, wavering, as whoever held it came nearer. She had to hide.

The only place she could think of, was in one of the cells. She walked towards where she'd remembered them. The only light now was a thin glow from the door to the corridor. If she stood with her back to the wall and near the cell door, anyone looking into the main room wouldn't see her. They could pass by. They would.

In almost complete darkness she walked into the nearest cell, her hands rubbing against the rough wall.

She held them in front of her, as she turned to the left. When she hit the side wall she was lucky she didn't bang her head against it. She felt the bricks brush her fringe. The voices were near now. She stood in the corner, feeling the wall with the tips of her fingers, then stood still, trembling slightly, waiting for whoever it was to pass.

The voices stopped.

Her heart was beating fast. Her neck muscles were tight. For a moment, she thought she couldn't breathe. She pressed back into the wall, could feel it rough and cold against her arms and back.

"Come out." A man's voice echoed, like a hammer blow into her brain "We have seen your little torch."

Light illuminated the cell, bright as daylight. Shadows rose and fell, dark angels sweeping the walls, as the torch beam moved across the doorway. Isabel clenched her fists, her nails biting deep into her skin. She would say she was looking for Sean. With a bit of luck, she'd just be in trouble for trespassing.

She turned and looked out the door. In a second, she knew she was in more trouble than just trespassing. A blond man, in a black jacket, was standing, beckoning her forward with a pale finger. Beside him stood two muscular guards in black uniforms. One of them had greasy black hair tied back in a ponytail. Each of them was cradling a menacing black machine pistol.

"You must be Isabel Ryan. I expected to find you in your hotel room, not here. You are more resourceful than we thought," said the man. A smile filled his face, as if finding Isabel was the best thing that had happened to him all day.

"The German police know I am here," said Isabel. There was sharp defiance in her tone, though dismay tugged at her.

"Thank you for telling us that," said the man. "Now, come on." He pointed at Isabel, looked at the guard to his right. His smile was a little wider now. He seemed to be enjoying himself.

"No, I won't," said Isabel. "And you'd better let me leave." But panic was rising from deep inside her. It felt as if she was at the bottom of a well, with no hope of rescue.

The man's laugh was crystal clear. It echoed off the brick walls. He said something fast in German to one of the guards. It sounded like a joke. The other man's face didn't change as he walked slowly towards Isabel. He slung his weapon on his shoulder, put his hands out wide, as if he was about to catch an animal.

"What the hell are you doing?" said Isabel.

"You will not cause any more problems." The man's words made Isabel's teeth clench. Her mouth went dry.

"Stay away from me." Isabel stepped back, but there was only the wall behind her.

"Did you know that thirty thousand German bodies ended up littering the streets above, to feed the birds in 1945? No, I expect not. No one cared for us then. Don't expect much sympathy now, Fraulein." He took a step forward, pointed at Isabel. "Move. I have no time left for you."

Isabel screamed. "Help!"

There was an answering shout almost immediately. It sent a bolt of hope through her, as if she'd seen a sudden light.

"Isabel!" It was Sean's voice. Faint, muffled, but unmistakeable!

The shock of hearing it made her step back.

The guards took hold of her arms, pushed her towards the door to the corridor. She stumbled. Then they were holding her arms tight, keeping her upright. They dragged her down the corridor and into another room. All she could think about now was Sean's voice. She'd heard it. He was alive!

Thank God!

The guards entered the main room behind her. Then there was another shout, louder this time. "Isabel."

Her heart literally jumped. Sean was near!

The man said something fast in German. The other guard patted her pockets, felt all over her body.

"Stop! Let me go," she shouted. Disgust swarmed though as they ground their hands along her thighs.

"Leave her alone." Sean's voice again, screaming.

They took her phone. Then they held her arms again.

She struggled. Their grip on her arms tightened. Then they pushed her forward and one guard put a key in a door, opened it inwards, fast. The other guard pushed her through the doorway.

Then Sean was holding her. Her heart almost stopped with the relief of being in his arms again.

The guards pulled the door closed behind them. There was no light in the room. The voices outside were faint now. Isabel and Sean just clung to each other, as if they'd been rescued from certain death. It took minutes for Isabel's elation at seeing him to subside.

"What the hell is going on?" she said. "What are you doing down here?" She touched the wall beside her. Its coldness and hardness made her close her eyes, as she wondered what would happen to them.

"Hell is right," said Sean. "I came down into this God-forsaken place to see if any of the work here had a connection to what happened to Eleni." He sounded rueful.

"What are they going to do with us?"

He didn't answer. He just kept holding her.

"They won't kill us, will they?" The words got stuck in her throat, came out only after a deep swallow.

"If they wanted to do that, they would have done it already." He sounded unrealistically positive. It wasn't very convincing.

"We'll find a way out," he said. He rubbed her back.

Isabel leaned into him. "I hope so." She asked him what had happened over the weekend.

"Let's sit down," said Sean. She could feel him trembling slightly as well, as if he was cold too.

"How long have you been down here?"

"Since Sunday afternoon," he said. "What day is it? My God, what time is it?"

"It's Monday, late afternoon."

They sat on the cold earth floor. He told her all about Eleni's death, Jerome's disappearance, the policeman who'd told him about the work at the cathedral. They figured out that it was the same man that Isabel had spoken to.

A mile-deep silence descended around them, whenever they stopped talking.

Neither of them sounded desperate any more, as if they were both trying to reassure the other. But the silence came back every time they stopped talking.

"We're dead if they leave us here, aren't we?" she said.

"There's no way they'll leave us."

She shivered again. It went right through her body like a wave.

He held her tight. "Maybe you can pick the lock."

"I don't have any tools."

"Let's find the door."

They sat facing each other with their shoulders rubbing up against the door.

"There's a breeze coming from the bottom," said Sean.

Isabel put her hand down. There was a small breeze. Then a noise, a soft thunk, echoed in the room beyond. Isabel felt her heart stop.

Someone was dragging something heavy across the floor.

46

Xena stood at the top of the stairs. She looked at her hand. There was a faint pink stain on her fingers. She put them to her lips. There was no smell of blood anymore and no iron taste.

She listened again, then went down the stairs. She had her knife in the palm of her hand, not visible, so anyone who came upon her wouldn't be alerted to any danger, but it was ready to slash across an unwary throat. She stopped after a while, listened again.

Nothing. Only the sound of dripping.

The next time she stopped it was because of another sound, the faint buzz of a motor running.

She paused, looked around for the haze of light that would tell her someone with a torch was following her. The gloom was intense. She waited, counted to ten, then lit her cigarette lighter, and examined the walls for wires. No doubt the people who Vanessa had employed to set up this dig had many ways to protect their presence, but perhaps they might be less vigilant than they might have been, with the need for haste.

She kept the lighter on as she went. When she reached the end of the stone corridor she went right, found a locked door, then an arch which led to another corridor. There was a faint light in the distance. She turned off her lighter.

The light was coming from a doorway. It was open a little. Then she heard a noise. The sound of whistling.

She put her eye to the edge of the doorway, looked into the room. A black- suited man was on his knees, mixing a tray with a mound of gray concrete powder on it. Beside him there was a pile of dusty red bricks. In front of him was an old wooden door. It looked as if he was about to brick it up.

There was another man. He was taller, with greasy black hair, tied back in a ponytail. He handed the first man a silver flask.

Xena moved her head back. Should she interrupt them? She smiled. Why not? She pulled one sleeve up, dragged her black jacket off one shoulder, then rubbed her hand against the slime near the bottom of the wall and spread some across her cheek. Then she groaned and shuffled her feet.

Nothing happened. She groaned louder, slumped against the wall and let her mouth open and her eyes half roll into her head. She turned away from the doorway, a grim determination, a steel wire of resolve, pushing away all doubts.

"Wer ist das?" a man's voice echoed.

A bright light struck her face. She blinked, half opened her eyes, rolled her head. The greasy-haired guard who held the torch had a stubby black Heckler & Koch MP5 in his other hand. The rounded safety button on the side was off.

The other man had left his brickwork and was standing to the side, also pointing an MP5 at her. She rolled her eyes back up in her head.

"Wer sind sie?" shouted the first man. He wanted to know who she was.

She groaned in response, got a hard poke in the shoulder from the barrel of a gun in reply. She restrained herself from slashing at him straight away, but her knife was tight in her palm behind her, its blade touching her skin reassuringly.

She had to put them properly off guard first.

She turned her face to the light, contorted it into an appeal, the sort of look they would expect from a refugee, sleeping rough. She put her left hand out, as if looking for money.

The second guard spat out the word "Flüchtling", refugee. The first aimed a kick at her, and shouted, "Raus!"

She fell sideways onto the stone floor, groaned, as if she was drunk. The greasy-haired guard laughed. She was drooling now, her mouth half open. She touched her chest, as if she was offering herself to them.

The greasy-haired guard said something fast. He reached down towards her. His gloves were thick, red and dirty with cement powder. She could see the white of his neck.

She slashed at his wind pipe, cutting it fast from side to side an inch deep. She continued moving the knife forward as she came to her feet.

The other guard's gun was coming up. Bullets were popping from it in a deafening burst. She twisted, lunged, jabbed with her knife at his throat. The tip went in only a half

Laurence O'Bryan

an inch, but it was enough. He lost focus on hitting her with the spray of bullets he had unleashed, and instinctively raised his hands to protect himself. She felt a bullet tug at her outspread jacket.

Anger surged through her. It was good to see blood flowing, to feel the strength of her rage, unfettered.

As he stepped back she jabbed twice. At his cheek bone, then slicing neatly into his pot belly. As she expected, his hands went in different directions, leaving his throat wide open again. She took a step closer to him, whispered, as she slashed the knife at his windpipe, feeling a grating reverberation as the blade sliced to his neck bone. It would take more than a slash to cut through the bone. But the man was dead already.

She turned. The guard who had kicked at her was holding his throat. His torch was rolling down the passage, casting shadows and waves of light as it spun. There was a coppery smell in the air. Blood was seeping through his hands, in gentle pulses. His eyes were wide. She could see the whites, like marble balls, staring at her. His legs were moving. He was pushing himself back against the wall, probably hoping to rise to his feet.

She would enjoy finishing this one.

She glanced around, saw no one, no other lights, stepped close to him, kneeled, leaned into his face.

He stopped moving. His eyes were pleading now. She kept her expression still. Then spat in his eye. As the phlegm landed she moved her fingers back along the handle of the

252

knife, so that the maximum possible length of blade would enter the next wound.

She slammed the blade deep and hard into the man's groin. His knees bent and a scream blubbered out of him, as the knife cut up through cloth and entered soft, yielding, flesh. It went so far, it probably entered his bladder, possibly it nicked his prostrate, which was good, and the reaction was exactly what she expected. He groaned, moved his hands from his throat. They shook wildly. Blood pumped down his chest, as if a tap had been opened.

She looked into his eyes, saw despair in all its weeping glory. The knowledge of approaching death, which no one can imitate, was in them. They bulged as the dying man gurgled again, suffering as he went.

She watched as his life force dimmed.

Thick gobs of blood, thrown around by his last twisting gasps, landed all over his face. She felt pure cold satisfaction. She'd been raped many times by men like this, lumbering brutes, who slapped and bruised and laughed, as they forced themselves into her.

Now it was her turn to laugh.

She did so, softly mocking as she stood up, then raised her fists in the air, tasting her moment of victory.

There was no doubt in her mind that the men would have raped her, if she had been weak. She was a beggar, a refugee to them. They might have killed her too. But she'd won.

Shouting broke out from the room they were outside. "Who's there?" a female voice cried.

"Help us!" a male voice called.

Laurence O'Bryan

She bent down, wiped her blade and her hands on the black jacket of the dead guard. This was turning into a good day. Not only had she tasted blood already, her revenge would be complete.

She held the knife in front of her as she walked into the room, holding the torch in her other hand, pointing it straight ahead.

47

Isabel gripped Sean's hand. They stopped shouting. The noise of the machine gun going off had reverberated through the cell, bouncing off the walls and vibrating the stones. Now the last echoes had gone and a light had returned to the room outside.

Then there was a woman's voice. "Who's there?"

The accent was foreign, faintly familiar. The hope that had entered Isabel's heart at the sound of the gunfire, the expectation that the police had arrived, and were about to rescue them was extinguished. All that was left was the light outside moving, the cold thumping in her heart, and Sean's hand squeezing hers even tighter.

"Who's there?" came the voice again. Light flashed along the millimetre-thick gap under the door and through the keyhole.

"Sean Ryan," said Sean. Then he leaned towards Isabel and whispered in her ear. "Get to the side. I'll rush her when she opens the door."

There was silence. The light stayed steady now under the door. A trickle of icy sweat ran down Isabel's back. Sean pushed at her, to force her to the side wall. Isabel's skin tingled. The sound of receding footsteps, though faint, echoed through the cell.

Were they being left down here?

Please.

No.

She reached towards the door. The wood was rough, hard, and impenetrable. It felt like the inside of a coffin. She pulled back her fist, held it steady. Should she hammer, plead? Would it be more dangerous to bring that person back, if she was actually intending to walk off?

She banged on the door.

"Don't leave us!" Her tone was angry, but inside something was clutching at her, telling her to stop.

If all the people who knew they were down here were dead, it could be a long time before anyone came down here again. You can die of thirst within a week. Your kidneys would be permanently damaged before that. They'd taught her about that painful fate in her kidnap training at the Foreign Office.

"Ssshhh," whispered Sean.

His hand gripped her shoulder. He was pushing her away to the side again. Isabel resisted, pushed back against him. If she waited, while Sean rushed out, he would be a target, literally, if whoever was out there decided to open their cell.

"We have to do it together," she whispered.

"I'm going first," he replied.

The sound of laughter echoed from beyond the door, as if they had been heard, whispering. Then the laughter stopped.

"Who is that?" whispered Isabel, leaning close to Sean.

There was a hesitation, then he replied, "I don't know."

Isabel was sure the sound of her breathing, and the deep tremble in it, could be heard beyond the door, it was that loud in her ears. It filled the darkness all around and echoed back through the walls and floor. Her cheeks felt hot too. And every muscle in her stomach had tightened, painfully. The voice had brought back memories, she didn't want to think about.

A scratching noise echoed from the other side of the door. It sounded as if an animal had been released. A metallic gleam appeared under the door.

"What the hell?" whispered Sean. "She's pushed something under the door."

Isabel moved her hand along the floor, slowly. She expected her fingertip would meet a sharp edge, some final torture for them.

Her finger touched something. She pulled her hand back quickly.

"What is it!" said Sean. She'd pushed against him.

"Wait," said Isabel.

"Let me try," said Sean.

She took a deep breath, tried to calm her thumping heart. "Sean, please. My fingers are smaller. Let me do it."

"No."

"Wait, Sean," she hissed.

She leaned down, moved her hand slowly along the bottom edge of the door, as if she was caressing a baby. A slight breeze tugged at her skin, like an animal breathing on her fingertips.

Then she touched something solid. She stopped breathing. What the hell was it? It had a round end. She pushed at it.

Then she knew.

"It's a key. She's pushed a key through to us." A rush of relief almost overcame her. Tears formed. Her chest tightened. Someone wanted to help them. Or was this another cruel game?

"Can you see the keyhole?"

She could. It was about the same size as the key she was holding. Please let the key fit. She raised it, put it into the hole, slowly. It turned, then stopped. A spike of anxiety twisted at her insides. Had it been a trick?

She tried the key again, pushing it backwards and forwards, slowly.

"It won't turn." Her voice was low.

"Let me try."

"Don't drop it."

She passed the key to him. Sean was breathing hard right beside her ear. Thank God she was facing this with him. She put her hand out, squeezed his arm.

"Try spitting on it," she said. She heard him spit, then try the key again. There was a long moment, when it seemed it wasn't going to work, then she heard a squeak. His arm rubbed against hers. The key was turning. It had to be.

"Thank God," said Sean. There was a louder squeak. He was opening the door. A rush of air hit her. There was a musty, metallic flavour, to it. There was no more light than before, but she knew the door was open.

"Were going to go, but slowly and carefully," he said.

"If we turn left in the corridor we can get the hell away from here. What were you thinking coming down here, Sean?"

"I was thinking about getting some answers."

"To what, for God's sake?"

"Why Eleni was murdered for a start."

"Did you find out?" It was obvious from her clipped tone that she was angry.

"I found out that they've been digging under this church trying to find something important."

"Come on, let's go." She gripped his arm. "That woman's voice made me very nervous."

They were padding across the room. The far door stood out against the blackness, as a paler shade of gray. There had to be light coming from somewhere up the corridor.

The air in the corridor felt warm. They turned left, went forward slowly.

As they moved, she relaxed for the first time in hours. They were going to get out of this stupid place. They were going home.

"What's that," whispered Sean.

Isabel's heart almost stopped. She'd bumped into something. It felt like a dead animal at her feet. And there was a light up ahead. It was seeping from a doorway at the far end of the corridor. She looked down. There was a bad smell here. A smell of shit and death. She could hear voices now. German voices.

"Let's go back," whispered Sean. "Maybe there's another way out."

He pulled at her hand. They walked faster this time, the darkness wasn't complete anymore, she could see the shadow of the wall. But her instincts told her to slow down. Her hand brushed the wall, and her throat tightened. Dread at what might lie ahead gripped her. Then the tunnel turned, and in a moment they were in total darkness again.

Sean slowed. The voices had stopped behind them. Whoever they were, they'd gone quiet. Then, up ahead, there was a sliver of light. It seemed to hang in the air. Isabel tugged at Sean's shirt.

He leaned close to her. She could feel his warmth on her ear when he whispered. "This is the room where they're doing that dig. They took me through it. I think they've broken through into something below."

"Can we get out this way?"

"I hope so."

"You hope so?!"

A faint glow seeped from all around the door. It was etching lines into Isabel's retina. Then there was a noise from the far side, a raised voice. She put her ear to the door. She could hear two voices.

"We have to go in there," whispered Sean. "This passage ends just beyond this. I saw it the last time I was here."

"Wait," said Isabel. "She's in there. The woman who pushed the key through to us."

Sean sighed. "Then she's a friend."

Isabel listened again, straining. Was Sean right?

Two women were talking in German. And then there was a scream.

She took hold of Sean's arm, which she could make out in the seeping light from the doorway, like a gray shadow beside her. The glow from the door was illuminating part of the floor too. It gave it a red tinge.

"Let's go back. I have a bad feeling about all this." A gnawing foreboding was building up inside her. She did not want to go any further. It was time to leave this place.

As she stepped back a grinding noise reverberated through the corridor and the door opened with a wash of light that blinded her. She put her hand over her eyes, stepped back.

"Come in. Join us," said the woman who'd pushed the key through to them. Isabel knew immediately she saw the woman's face that she'd been right about the voice being familiar, even though it was years since they'd met. Memories of their meeting, under Manhattan, with dead bodies all around, came back to her.

They were motioned forward.

"Do not make any mistakes, Sean Ryan, or I will blow your wife's brains all over your face."

Isabel stepped forward. Her eyes were recovering. She was in a square stone-roofed room. The walls were dark, stained black high up, green nearer the floor.

There were small niches in the walls and a raised stone area at the far end. Rough-cut chunks of stone were piled up along the walls.

Two men, dressed in black, one of them wearing a red helmet, were slumped against the far wall. There was a lot of blood around them. A digging machine with a yellow arm stood near the raised area. Propped up against it, with her back against its side, was a woman with blond hair. As Isabel watched the woman tried to move, but her mouth opened in obvious pain as she did. There was blood on her clothes. A lot of it.

"Xena," the woman screamed. "You will not find it!" She coughed and leaned back.

Isabel took a step towards the woman. "Oh my God, what have you done?" She turned to Xena. Her voice was shaking. She tried to make it sound firm. "We have to call an ambulance."

The muzzle of Xena's gun was pointing at Isabel. She closed the door behind them, slid a two-inch thick iron bolt into the stone of the wall to lock it.

"We will," said Xena. "When I have what I came here for."

"What they hell are you talking about?" said Isabel.

"There is something in that hole. And you've arrived right on time to help me get it out."

"What the hell could be worth all these lives?" shouted Isabel, waving at the bodies. She looked at Sean, moved her head sideways a millimetre, indicating for him to go around the room, so Xena couldn't keep them both covered.

Sean moved slowly away from Isabel.

"Go and look in the hole, Sean," said Xena. "And don't try anything stupid, or your wife will be dead. You know I will do it." She raised her gun, sighted along the barrel at Isabel.

"See the channels cut in the stone beneath your feet?" Her voice was firm, commanding.

Isabel looked down. Thin grooves, in a pattern like the rays of the sun, headed towards the end of the room, to the hole Sean was now walking towards. Now he was looking into it.

"Rush the witch," hissed the injured woman beside Isabel. She looked up at Isabel and smiled. It would have looked like a pleasant smile, but there was blood on the woman's teeth and lips.

"Have a good look, Sean. You are curious about what happened to your friends, aren't you?" Xena's tone softened. "Vanessa has always been unhappy with people interfering, but there is nothing she can do about it any more."

Sean bent forward, peered into the hole.

"Remember, I can put a neat little hole in your wife's skull any moment I want to."

Xena's gun, a small black pistol, had H&K embossed in black on its side. She took a step towards Isabel. She was ten feet from her now.

"My aim is very good."

Isabel stared at her. Her mouth was dry, her neck and face muscles tightening with the thought of what would happen if Xena pulled the trigger.

Xena had a half-smile on her face. She stepped back. "And don't listen to anything that Nazi bitch tells you. She wouldn't care if you all died in agony. All she wants to do is destroy what's down here."

Sean went down into the opening in the floor. Only his head was visible.

"This is weird," he said.

Xena went towards him.

There would be a moment to rush her, but Isabel would have to time it right. She followed them, looked into the hole.

A landslide of rock stretched away below for thirty feet, down to a larger room – this one with the same structure, and the same circular pattern carved on the floor, the same grooves like rays leading to a ten-foot-wide red circle at its centre, but this time they were deeper, as if they had some practical use, that they weren't just a decoration. Sean was scrambling down the rocks. He reached the bottom, turned, gave Isabel a nod.

"Go down. Join him," said Xena. She was still pointing the gun at Isabel.

"What the hell's down there?" Isabel didn't move. Here tone was defiant. Maybe if she argued with Xena, Sean might have a chance to get away down there.

She blinked. The light above their heads came from fluorescent tubes in the ceiling. They looked like something out of the mid-20th century. Xena walked towards a set of light switches near a door at the far end of the room. She turned most of the lights off, leaving only one set on above the hole. Much of the upper room was in shadow now.

Xena walked to the injured woman. She looked up at Xena, a sneer on her face. Xena closed the gap between them, pulled her arm back, slammed the butt of her gun into the side of Vanessa Sheer's head. The noise of cracking bone was loud, sickening. Vanessa grunted. Her head slumped forward. Blood oozed from her forehead.

"That will keep her quiet." Xena turned to Isabel. "I don't need you," she said, pointing her gun at Isabel again. "It might be good for your husband to see your blood flow down those channels."

Isabel's hands became fists. She could imagine the fiery agony of a bullet wound. "Okay," she shouted. She followed Sean. It was like going down a stone avalanche. As she went down the rest of the room below came into view.

Its walls were a circle of rough gray stone. There were smooth pillars of black rock all around the room. The pillars had wolf's heads carved into them. Some were snarling. Others had something clenched between their teeth.

She joined Sean near a large red circle in the floor at the centre of the room. It looked like the lens of a giant unblinking eye. There was a darker red circle at its centre, with something carved into it.

"The wolves on those pillars show the faces of Fenrir. It's foretold in German mythology that he will kill Odin at the end of time," said Sean.

"What the hell is Fenrir doing down here?" said Isabel. She looked back the way she'd come. Shadows were moving around the walls. Xena was joining them. She had a torch in her hand.

"Fenrir had to be tied up by the old gods." Sean walked towards a pillar. Isabel walked to one on the far side of the room.

"Maybe this is where they tied him up. They say that if he ever breaks free it will be the end of the world."

A thunderous banging noise came from the room above.

As the echoes faded Xena waved the gun at Sean. "Come here to the eye, Sean. Move."

Isabel stepped towards her. "What the hell's so important down here that you'll kill us all for it?"

Xena stared, wide-eyed at her. Her skin was glistening in the torchlight. Her cheekbones prominent.

"You will find out soon enough."

"What the hell is this about?" Isabel's reply was almost a scream.

Sean was walking slowly towards Xena. As he got closer Xena turned fast. "Stop," she shouted. She swung the gun up to point at Isabel's face. Isabel stood still. Another bang sounded from the room above. This time dust came from the ceiling.

Xena was standing close to her now, only a few feet away.

"If you try anything I will make her suffer. You have one chance, Sean. Do what I say, if you want to protect your lovely wife."

Sean was behind Isabel now. She could shoot them both dead with a few twitches of her trigger finger.

"Move, Sean!" shouted Xena. "Get the stone from the centre of the eye."

"What the hell?" screamed Isabel, turning to look at Xena.

"He will do what I say." Xena shouted, sighted along the barrel from Sean to Isabel, moving the gun fluidly, as if she was well used to using it.

"Stop it. I'll do it," said Sean.

He looked at Isabel, shook his head, as if telling her not to try anything. "Don't worry." He smiled. Then he stood at the edge of the circle, placed one foot onto it. "It's as solid as a rock."

Isabel went towards him, her breath catching in her throat, as he walked slowly, spreading his legs and his weight, as he went across the red disk.

"What the hell is this place?" she said, in a low hissing tone, turning to face Xena.

"It's the place General Patton was looking for when he dug up half this city in the summer of forty-five," said Xena.

Sean was moving slowly, steadily. It seemed as if there was nothing to be concerned about. He bent down as he neared the centre of the slightly-arched red circle. "What was he looking for, the Holy Grail?" said Sean.

"No," said Xena.

Sean was looking down. He was frowning.

"My God," said Sean. He looked puzzled, as he peered down at the disk. "There's something beneath us."

Another echoing boom sounded from the room up above. Then it came again. Dust drifted in the air around them. Someone was trying to break into the room up above.

Isabel shivered. "This place feels cursed," she said, looking at the walls around them.

"This place is cursed," said Xena. She was at the edge of the disk, opposite Isabel. She put a foot on it, as if she was considering walking to where Sean was.

"Don't!" said Sean. "This doesn't feel stable!" He sounded alarmed.

"What do you see?" said Xena. She put her foot onto the disk.

"Stop!" said Isabel.

She wanted Sean to come back, to get off this stupid disk. There was something strange about this whole place. She held her hand out towards him, swallowed hard. Something was rising inside her throat, tightening it.

"Don't worry," said Sean, again.

"What do you see?" shouted Xena. She slid her foot forward.

"There's a metal tube in the hole in the centre."

"Get it," said Xena.

Sean reached down, touched the disk. "It's stuck. Find something sharp to help me dig it out." He swung around to face them.

Xena reached down her leg, extracted a black six-inch blade from a sheath on her thigh. She slid it across the disk towards Sean. He reached towards the knife. As he did, Isabel heard a faint rumble.

"Come back," said Isabel. "This is too dangerous. We don't know what's under this." She glared at Xena.

Xena was staring at the centre of the disk, her attention focused on Sean's hand.

He raised the knife that Xena had slid to him, held it in the air, then looked over at Isabel. "There's a strange noise coming from beneath this," he said. He shook his head from side to side, trying to tell her something.

Fear pressed into Isabel's stomach like a slab of cold stone. She reached towards him, her fingers outstretched.

"Get it," shouted Xena.

Sean stabbed the knife down at the centre point of the disk. A faint cracking sound could be heard.

48

Henry Mowlam watched as the two burly, bullet-proof-jacketed officers wielded their red battering rams against the door. Their combined effort was having little effect. The door was barely marked.

The Kriminalkommissar of the Nuremberg police, Kurt Dienelt, shrugged. "We will use the Semtex, ja?"

"You have the new C17B, I hope," said Henry.

"Ja C17B and C18," replied Kurt.

Henry nodded. A limited explosive field was what was needed. They didn't want to kill everyone in there. But whatever the Nuremberg police had brought with them had to be used fast. Tunnels, he'd found out, dating back to medieval times, connected most of the old parts of Nuremberg. Some led to the nearby Pegnitz River.

The tracking data from the phone he had given Isabel had led them here. He had also managed to speed up a search for Sean's last known mobile location, which had been lost in some endless German request and approval loop. The matching location data had enabled him to persuade this German detective that an immediate armed search was necessary.

The discovery of blood soaked bodies in the room further back had confirmed that Henry Mowlam wasn't an intelligence officer, masquerading as a conspiracy nut.

An officer with a bulky utility belt and a triangular red patch on each arm, whispered something in the Kommissar's ear.

"Come. We must go back thirty feet," said Kurt, in a tone that left no doubt who he thought was in charge of the operation.

Henry nodded. This was not the time for arguments. They walked fast back along the corridor. Security cooperation between the Federal Republic of Germany and the United Kingdom, had been a delicate matter for the last few years, but things had improved recently, due to hard work on both sides.

Henry had been given permission to come to Nuremberg by the most senior person in Her Majesty's Foreign Office he had ever dealt with. The permission had come with a warning not to cause trouble. Fortunately, that gave him a wide brief.

He stood, his back to the wall, out of sight of the door they were trying to get through. Further along the wall, behind them, were ten heavily-armed officers that the Kommissar had rounded up, all members of the Spezialoperationen Unit.

"We are ready, ja?" said Kurt. He nudged Henry.

Henry nodded, closed his eyes and opened his mouth to limit any shockwave damage to his teeth.

The explosive wave was larger than he had anticipated. It passed through him, making his body feel like jelly, shaking the earth like water. His eardrums reverberating as he watched the Spezialoperationen Unit members run forward into the cloud of dust further up the corridor, their helmet lights illuminating the dust, turning it yellow.

Each of them had large black thermal vision goggles below dull black helmets. If there was anyone alive beyond the door they would find them quickly.

49

A snarling, grinding filled the room. Her vision danced. Everything in front of her shifted, as if the ground was buckling. For one mad moment Isabel thought Fenrir was rising from the depths.

"Isabel," Sean screamed. She moved forward, though every instinct was telling her to step back.

A whoosh sounded. Air was being sucked from the room. Dust whirled. The grinding stopped, echoing into the walls. Her mouth opened. In place of the red disk where Sean had stood, a hole gaped. She peered into it. Perhaps twenty feet below, dark reddish water thundered. She got down on her knees, touched the smooth edge of the hole, her hand shaking.

"Sean!" she screamed, fear descending like a heavy shroud around her.

"Sean," she screamed again.

Hands dragged her back by the ankles and calves. She clawed for the edge, but could not hold it. She twisted. Two burly men in black police uniforms held her.

"Bitte," said one. She struggled violently to break free.

Laurence O'Bryan

Henry Mowlam stepped forwards.

Isabel shouted at him. "Henry! Sean's down there – you have to get ladders, ropes…"

Henry stepped past her, peered into the hole. "I'm sorry, Mrs Ryan. We'll have to wait for an underwater rescue team."

Her body shook. She went from side to side, trying to break free. She struck out. The black gloved hands didn't release her. Red dust filled the air. She coughed. She was watching her life slip away in slow motion as she was pulled back from the hole.

"Sean," she screamed. She pushed forward, struggling. The men holding her went with her, their grip on her arms and shoulders, tight, but moving along her arms, as she twisted away from them.

Anxiety gripped her tight, as she knelt near what had been the red disk. The gaping circular hole looked like the entrance to a large well. A circle of brick side walls was visible. Below, the water was running fast, like the skin of a snake passing. The red disk had been a lid over an entrance to an underground river. Isabel leaned forward to try to see Sean.

She couldn't.

"Sean." Her voice echoed down towards the water. Tears slipped from her eyes. Her chin quivered.

The fast moving current was taking the water out of sight, constantly. Then something slid across the surface of the water and a tail appeared, just for a moment. It thrashed and disappeared. She screamed.

"No!" Another tail appeared. And another. They were all heading for the same spot in the river. The hair on her back rose.

"No!" Her scream echoed. Terror gripped her, a vice squeezing every muscle in her body.

She heard a shout in German. They wanted her to move away from the hole.

"Isabel, is Sean definitely down there?" said Henry Mowlam.

She nodded her head. There was only one thing for it. She had to dive in after him. To hell with what was down there. There wasn't much time left. He must have been knocked out. He could be just there.

She had to dive in.

She bent to take her shoes off, struggling against the men holding her. She fumbled at her laces, fear and shock making her fingers seem pudgy and powerless.

The hands holding her gripped tighter. She looked up. Two burly German policemen with black helmets were shaking their heads.

"Let me go!" she shouted.

She yanked violently at the men, twisting and turning in their grasp. Her desperation almost succeeded. Then Henry was holding her shoulders too. She had no hope against three of them.

"Henry, you have to let me go down there. Please. He might be alive. Please!" Her face was contorted. A wave of panic rose up through her and sent her chin trembling, tears rushing from her eyes.

"I'm sorry, Mrs Ryan. You cannot go down there. It's far too dangerous. I wouldn't even let a trained diver into that." Henry held her shoulders tight, turned her forcefully to him.

"Was there anyone else here?"

Isabel nodded.

He looked towards the hole. "Maybe there's a way out down there. We might find him."

He was being optimistic. She looked away. Tears were falling down her face. Memories of all she'd been through with Sean filled her mind. The day they'd met in Istanbul. The day they got married. Their son waiting for them. What would she tell Alek?

She bent over. Her chest shook as more tears came. They weren't just for herself. She tried to slide gently from the hands holding her.

Another face was in front of her. It was a German policeman's. He had blue eyes, brown hair and an honest open expression.

"Do not go near that hole. This underground river runs away from the Peignitz. There are catfish down there. They are dangerous. Come, you must leave now. Come."

Isabel managed one last look. What she saw made her stomach twist.

There was something moving on the stone wall of the hole. Giant gray slugs. The wall was covered in them. They'd been invisible because of their colour. She bent forward, vomited.

The hands that were holding her released her for half a second. Then there was a voice calling her.

"Isabel." She fell forward. She didn't care where she fell. One thought filled her mind, as the world turned to darkness.

Sean was gone.

Epilogue

Isabel opened her eyes. There was white everywhere. She closed them. Buzzing filled her ears, low, insistent. She opened her eyes again. The buzzing was an alarm on a piece of glittering electrical equipment on a high white stand beside her.

There was a face looming over her. It was Henry Mowlam's.

"You gave us quite a scare," he said.

"How long have I been here?"

"A few hours. You banged your head after you blacked out. I lost my bloody temper with those Germans too. They should have been holding you a bit tighter." He put a hand on her arm, squeezed it.

A gnawing emptiness filled her up as she remembered what had happened to Sean. Tears threatened, then fell. She wiped at them fats, brushing them away.

"You didn't find him, did you? Did you?"

Henry's mouth opened, closed. He shook his head. "They should find his body today. They're searching an underground cave the river flows into."

"What kind of a stupid place was that?" She bent her head, out her fists in her eyes.

278

"Apparently that lower room has been hidden for decades. It's a lot older than the one above it." He stopped.

She put her hands down, gripped the sheet. "There was something important down there. Sean was trying to reach it. He was forced to go over that hole. Did you find Xena?"

He looked at her for a long moment, as if deciding what to tell her. Then he shrugged. "We didn't find anyone else. Just three bodies in the room above."

She looked away. Had there been time for Xena to escape? Had she fallen in after Sean? A long window with thin white blinds filled the wall to her right. They were closed tight.

"How did you end up down there?" said Henry.

She shook her head, closed her eyes. Nothing mattered anymore. Sean was gone. Everything was gone. She didn't want to live. But she had to, for Alek's sake.

"I found a steel canister in that room you were in," said Henry. He spoke slowly. "It had a Nazi symbol embossed on it."

"What was in it?" Isabel put her head up. Was this what Xena had been looking for? Had Sean thrown it aside as he fell?

"I'm not at liberty to tell you."

Her hand shook as she pointed at him. "My husband might have died for that. You have to tell me what he gave his life for." Her voice was shrill. She bit her lip.

The hum of the fluorescent light above their heads filled the room as she waited for his answer.

"Tell me, Henry. I need to know he didn't die in vain."

Henry glanced towards the door.

"There were letters in it."

"What letters?"

He sighed. "I suppose it will all come out, eventually. The letters are from Pope Pius XII to Adolf Hitler. I took pictures of them before the head of the operation on the German side took them away. I was lucky he didn't stop me." He looked surprised.

"He's one of the good guys. I've had them translated from German. The letters express Pius X11's support for Hitler's policies towards the Jews, and encourage him to wage war on Soviet Russia immediately. They are dated from well before Hitler's invasion of Russia. It's all in diplomatic language, of course, but it's clear that the pope at that time supported what Hitler was doing." He paused. "I'm sure they'll be disputed though."

She spoke slowly now. "That's so sick. How could he have supported Hitler?"

Henry shrugged. "If Hitler followed what the pope suggested, that probably led to him losing the war, Mrs Ryan. If he'd kept to his treaty with Stalin, the Normandy landings would have failed or they'd never have happened."

She stared at him. "My grandfather committed suicide after working at the Nuremberg trials. He claimed that many on the German side, who should have been tried, weren't. I don't care what might have happened. All I know is what did happen. Hitler murdered millions of men, women and children." Anger rose inside her.

She put her palms to her eyes. Tears were flowing again. She couldn't stop them now. How stupid she'd been to let Sean come here.

"Sean won't have given his life in vain," said Henry, softly.

"We suspected someone was behind the deaths of refugees here in Germany, by infecting them deliberately. The woman whose body was down in that first room, has been linked to a doctor who was also murdered. He worked at a facility she was involved with. It appears they were both part of a plot to mass murder refugees. Sean helped to stop that. He brought you and the German authorities down on them. I expect there will be more arrests too."

She didn't care. Sean was gone. Gone for ever. How could that be? A sharp pain of emptiness made her bend forward.

She tried to get some words out, but they faltered, turned to dust in her mouth. A minute later, after the quiet sobs had passed, the words came. "What were they looking for down there, just those letters?"

Henry nodded. "Probably. I expect they had a plan for how to use them." His voice was strong, but he spoke the words slowly. At the end he pressed his lips together.

"I want to be alone," said Isabel. She turned away, closed her eyes. A few seconds later she heard the click of the door closing. She put her head to the hard, starched, pillow.

Then the nightmares came. Sean's face. His voice, calling

her. He was floating in the water, looking up at her. There was something rippling at the surface. Xena's face broke through the water.

Isabel screamed.

Thank you for taking the time to read *The Nuremberg Puzzle*.

If you enjoyed it **please tell your friends and post a review** on Amazon.

Go here to do that: http://SmartUrl.it/Puzzle4

Your review is **important** to me. Reviews help books to sell.

All reviews are appreciated.

Thank you, Laurence O'Bryan.

You can see **the other books in the series,** read posts and **comment** at: http://lpobryan.com/blog/

You can also **follow me on Facebook**:

https://www.facebook.com/laurenceobryanauthor

Made in the USA
Middletown, DE
04 April 2017